Had he been

For an instant sh—
erupted into mot—
cramped space. Her heart slammed in her chest
when she saw blood trickling down the side of his
face.

"Stay down," he hissed.

She breathed again. He was alive. "How bad are you
hurt?"

"I'm fine. We've got to move."

"But you're bleeding!"

As she said it, the blood reached his right eye and
he swiped at it, winced, but it seemed more in
annoyance than pain.

"We've got to move," he repeated. "He knows we're
here, and it sounds like he's using high-velocity
rounds, so this isn't going to be a shelter after all."

He was clearly coherent and aware, so she shelved
her immediate panic. "Move to where?"

He was silent for a moment, clearly thinking. Hetty
tried not to move, which was difficult. What was
more difficult was ignoring the feel of Spence's body
pressing down on her.

Dear Reader,

It took only one word to get me to agree to writing the book that would launch this new Coltons series. Beyond that, I found the pairing of a rugged backcountry guide and a seaplane pilot fascinating. Not only because the work itself interests me, but because of their backstory.

The Colton books are always a challenge, melding your own individual storyline with the overall arc of the entire series. You learn a lot about cooperation and how other authors work. And you learn to truly appreciate the tremendous efforts of the editing staff who have to oversee it all and make sure it all fits and makes sense. That is not a job I would want!

Oh, and that one word that sold me? Very simple.

Alaska.

All I heard was Coltons of Alaska, and I was in. Just the name stirs me, and writing about the kind of people who are tough enough to make it their home was a delight. I hope that comes through in the reading.

Enjoy the adventure!

Justine Davis

COLTON IN THE WILD

JUSTINE DAVIS

ROMANTIC SUSPENSE

Special thanks and acknowledgment are given to Justine Davis for her contribution to The Coltons of Alaska miniseries.

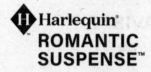

Harlequin®
ROMANTIC SUSPENSE™

Recycling programs for this product may not exist in your area.

ISBN-13: 978-1-335-47151-2

Colton in the Wild

Harlequin Enterprises ULC
22 Adelaide St. West, 41st Floor
Toronto, Ontario M5H 4E3, Canada
www.Harlequin.com

Printed in Lithuania

MIX
Paper | Supporting responsible forestry
FSC® C021394

Justine Davis lives on Puget Sound in Washington State, watching big ships and the occasional submarine go by and sharing the neighborhood with assorted wildlife, including a pair of bald eagles, deer, a bear or two, and a tailless raccoon. In the few hours when she's not planning, plotting or writing her next book, her favorite things are photography, knitting her way through a huge yarn stash and driving her restored 1967 Corvette roadster—top down, of course.

Connect with Justine on her website, justinedavis.com, at X.com/justine_d_davis or at Facebook.com/justinedaredavis.

Books by Justine Davis

Harlequin Romantic Suspense

The Coltons of Alaska

Colton in the Wild

The Coltons of Owl Creek

A Colton Kidnapping

Cutter's Code

Operation Second Chance
Operation Mountain Recovery
Operation Whistleblower
Operation Payback
Operation Witness Protection
Operation Takedown
Operation Rafe's Redemption

Visit the Author Profile page
at Harlequin.com for more titles.

This one is for all the people of the glorious, beautiful and amazing state of Alaska, which is at the very top of my wish list of places to visit. I hope my admiration comes through and that any mistakes are minor enough for you to forgive.

Chapter 1

Spence Colton was just too pretty for his own good.

This wasn't the first time Hetty Amos had had that thought, and this likely wasn't going to be the last time, but it was just as annoying every time.

And, just as usual, the client flirting with him now only cared about his good looks—she didn't actually care about *him*. Hetty understood, to an extent. With his thick, dark brown hair and bright blue eyes, and that six-foot muscular form radiating a subtle power built by years of an essentially athletic sort of work—hiking, skiing, paddling—he was nothing short of eye-catching.

So, yeah, she understood. She just didn't like it.

She'd watched the dance between him and attractive female clients so many times she should be numb to it by now. She didn't know—not for sure anyway—if he ever took any of them up on their blatant offers. Didn't want to know. Because, of course, she had absolutely, utterly, definitely no interest in the guy's love life. None whatsoever. He was simply someone she had to work with. Had to put up with, even with his annoyingly juvenile habit of flirting right back at female clients…and maybe more.

Had to, because Spence wasn't just the premier guide

of her employer, Rough Terrain Adventures. RTA was the number-one tour company in Shelby, and one of the top-ranked in the entire state of Alaska. And Spence was also a part owner of the business. He was the son of Ryan Colton, one of the two founding brothers of the company. He was someone she had to get along with, since they often had to work together. As a pilot who specialized in getting to the more remote places—RTA's bread and butter—she needed to stay on good terms with the star. And that required pretty much ignoring Spence outside of work.

Which was easy, because she had no interest in him outside of work at all. None whatsoever.

The denial rang hollow even in her mind.

"—be sure and look me up when you come to LA!"

"I'll do that, next time I set foot there."

Hetty wondered if the woman even noticed the undertone in his voice. Or maybe she was only imagining it, being the one here who knew Spence would hike to the Bering Strait before he'd set that foot in Los Angeles.

The unquestionably lovely blonde finished sending her phone number to Spence's cell phone from her own, smiled brilliantly at him, lifted the phone to snap a final photo of him and actually giggled as she turned away and headed for the car waiting to pick her up and her thankfully much more reserved girlfriend.

Spence was grimacing now, but Hetty was certain he'd look great in the photo. Because he always did. Other people looked silly when caught off guard, or had some unflattering expression on their face—she tended to a brow-furrowed, mouth-twisting, wry expression herself—but not Spence. Never Spence. No matter the angle, the lighting, or the situation, he always managed to look like he'd stepped off the cover of some men's magazine. Something about the bone structure of his face, especially when lit up by his signature flirtatious grin, got almost any female thinking appreciative—and often racy—thoughts.

But not her. Never her. All he did for her was spark her temper, which was already on a short leash.

Still, she watched as he ran a finger down a page then signed off on the paperwork for the enamored client and put it in a folder for Lakin to get to when she could. Which would be soon, Hetty was sure; Lakin Colton was her friend and Spence's cousin—not to mention her brother's girl-friend—and Hetty knew she was both quick and efficient.

Then he went back to his phone, fingers swiping it open then tapping on the screen. And out of nowhere the snark arose and the words were out before she could think better of them.

"Going to call her already?"

She saw his fingers pause. Then he went back to tapping and, without looking at her, said flatly, "Deleting."

She felt her cheeks heat and she hated herself for giving in to the urge to make that wisecrack. But then it struck her to wonder if that was what he always did when one of those female clients—and for all she knew maybe a few males, too—insisted on giving him their number.

Deep down, she wanted to believe it. To believe that all this silliness and flirting was just on the surface. To believe that underneath all that, he still had the depth of the Spence she'd known in school. The Spence she'd once worked with so closely but could now hardly stand to be in the same room with.

The Spence who had needed her then but now saw her as merely another RTA employee.

The fact that she missed the days of him needing her was like salt poured over an open wound. She had everything she'd ever dreamed of. She'd worked hard, studied, gone to flight school as she ached to do ever since, as a child, she'd looked upward to see float or seaplanes traversing the wide-open Alaska skies. Since the state had more registered pilots than any other, it happened often. The family story was that, from the first, as a toddler, Hetty would reach toward the aircraft, as if she wanted to snag one for herself.

And now she had. True, she didn't own the Cessna 206. RTA did. But she was the only one who flew it, except for Will Colton occasionally. Spence's uncle had been RTA's fixed-wing pilot back in the early days, flying his old single-engine Beaver, and still kept his hand in by taking flights now and then. But for the most part, the Cessna was hers and she saw to it with the intensity of the experienced pilot that she was, who loved the plane that let her fly.

And if that meant she had to put up with the irritation to her soul that Spence Colton was, then so be it.

She hated him.

She hated him, and the sooner he admitted that, at least to himself, the better. Spence didn't blame her. And in fact, he should count it a success. After all, didn't he go overboard with attractive clients for precisely that reason? Sure, he'd always been a bit of a flirt, he admitted that. It was a skill he'd developed early in his life when he'd seen it work. It diverted people. Kept them from pushing into areas he preferred to keep well-hidden.

Now, he also did it because he knew it annoyed Hetty. And he needed to keep that safe distance between them.

But the safe distance he'd wanted had turned into a gulf he doubted he could ever be bridged. And he hadn't anticipated how much that would bother him.

Brilliant, Colton. Work hard to keep your distance then whine about her being unreachable.

Maybe the brain quirk that made it hard for him to read like other people had screwed up more than just that. But thinking of it only reminded him of why he was able to function at all with such a quirk. There was one reason: the tutor who had discovered a way for him to utilize his memory and his ability to visualize and convert that talent into his atypical version of reading. It worked, and it had saved him.

True, he had kept to his decision not to go on to college. He'd been relieved just to make it through high school with decent grades—although much better than decent in math classes—thanks to that tutoring. He'd never been hot on the college idea anyway. He knew, had known from childhood, what he'd wanted to do with his life. And now he was doing it, spending his days exploring this place he so loved. And if the people he was leading on these explorations weren't always as appreciative as he was, he just considered it the price he had to pay to do what he wanted to do.

As for the women, if they flirted, he flirted back. If they were single. He might be a bit loose with one-on-one teasing, but that was a line he would not cross. Of course, he could only take their word for that single status. When one suggested—or outright demanded—that it go further, he wiggled his way out. Because for him the banter was the end of it. His family might worry about it, to the point of them strongly suggesting he never do any trips without someone else along, but to him it meant nothing. In fact, the game was a bit taxing these days, but that was because Hetty was usually his pilot when a trip required a plane. And keeping up the front when she was there was much harder.

He'd catch her watching him with those amazing green eyes, not even bothering to hide her disgust. It stabbed at him, painfully, but he kept going. Because, in the end, that was the goal. The more Hetty disliked him, the easier it was for him to keep his distance. So yeah, he might go a little far with the flirting, but it was for a good cause.

Because Hetty Amos was not for the likes of him.

"How'd it go?"

The call from the hallway leading to the office wing of the RTA headquarters broke through his miserable thoughts and turned him around.

Uh-oh. Both of them?

He might be the premier, most-requested guide at RTA, but Ryan and William Colton *were* RTA. His father and uncle had founded the business nearly three decades ago. They had both pulled back a little now, especially since his cousin Parker had stepped into the main management role, but they essentially were still RTA. It wouldn't exist without them. And he would likely be stuck doing some other job he'd hate because it would be hard for him. He could do it, thanks to the tricks that tutor had taught him more than a decade ago, but he wouldn't like it.

And he certainly wouldn't like it the way he treasured

every minute of being out in the wilds of this state that was a part of his soul.

So, in a way, he owed this life that gave him so much enjoyment to that long-ago tutor. That teenaged girl who had taken the job so seriously, worked so hard at it. That tutor who had realized the contradiction in the fact that he was great at math but sucked at word-based math problems, and had made the intuitive leap that had helped him go from floundering to being able to get through. That tutor who had taught him how to apply his knack for visualizing things to words and letters and sounds, enabling him to read so much easier, even if it was in a way that was different than most people. That tutor who had showed him how to function in a world where he wasn't the norm.

That tutor who had, in essence, saved him.

That tutor named Hetty Amos.

Chapter 2

"Great," Spence belatedly answered his father's question about how this last trip had gone.

"Come on back to the office," Uncle Will said.

Spence wondered if a lecture was in the offing. Maybe Hetty had complained about Ms. Merchant. He discarded that thought immediately. She wouldn't do that. She might call him out to his face, as she just had, but she wouldn't complain behind his back. It just wasn't her way.

He stepped through the door into the RTA manager's office, which these two men had once shared but was now staked out and claimed by Will's son, Parker, who was currently out on a short morning trip himself. Parker kept his hand in on the guide side, not just the business side. Spence didn't envy his cousin. As good as he himself was with numbers, the manager's job seemed daunting. Probably because there was a lot of reading involved, which he could do—thanks to Hetty—but didn't like much. Not that he didn't like books and stories, he did, but audio was his method of choice for consuming them. Which reminded him he wanted to finish the book he'd started a couple of days ago. And then—

"—would you suggest?"

Damn, he'd tuned out. He glanced at Uncle Will but then focused on his father, who had spoken. He'd put on a little weight since he'd semiretired, although it seemed to Spence he wasn't relaxing, not when he was regularly trekking out for his day-long fishing trips. There was only a touch of gray hair at his temples and his blue eyes—the ones Spence had inherited—were as bright and lively as ever. If it wasn't for the frequent hints that he would like to be a grandfather sometime soon, he'd be the perfect father figure.

He is the perfect father figure. You're the one who's out of step.

"Sorry, Dad. I was thinking how much I'd hate doing any other job, so if you're going to fire me, I don't want to hear it."

His father snorted audibly, but Will laughed outright. Spence smiled at his uncle, just slightly more salt-and-peppered than his father but with the same blue eyes. Also semiretired yet seemingly unable to slow down, he worked as hard at promoting Aunt Sasha's pottery business as he had when he'd helped run RTA full-time.

"Like we'd fire the most in-demand guide in the state of Alaska," Uncle Will said, still chuckling.

Spence shifted his feet, gave his uncle a crooked grin. "Not quite. Maybe in Shelby."

"Ha. I've read the reviews, son," Dad said. "You're going to top that statewide list before you're through."

"So," Uncle Will said, "now that we've cleared that up, back to the question."

"Uh…which was?" Spence asked.

"Your father and I are in need of a good spot for a nice,

long day of fishing, now that we've survived the Fourth of July rush."

Spence blinked. The holiday rush wasn't over for him, by a long shot, but he was more puzzled by the question.

"You're asking me?"

They both had lived here longer than he'd been alive. Not by much, true, but still…they knew the local environs as well as anyone, and better than most.

"We know all the usual spots," his uncle said. "But we want someplace we've never been."

"For a nice, long, uninterrupted day," Dad said pointedly.

"And productive, fishwise," put in Uncle Will.

"And scenic." Dad again.

"And private."

"And a ways out there—"

"I get it, I get it," Spence said, laughing now. "You want a day where nobody will find you or bother you or ask you to talk or expect anything trickier than reeling in a ton of fish."

Both men grinned at him. "Exactly."

"I knew you'd get it," Dad added. "It'll be our last chance before things start getting really hectic for the rest of the summer. So you know a spot that meets all that criteria?"

Spence grinned back. "Most of Alaska?" he suggested.

"Yeah, yeah," Uncle Will said. "But specifically? We know the closer-in spots, but they've gotten a bit more populated than we'd like for this. Hence we ask Mr. No Place Too Far."

Spence couldn't deny he felt a bit flattered that these two men, of all people, were asking him where to go.

"You want to hike in or fly?"

"Weather looks good for the next week, so I can fly us

in, in the company helicopter," Dad said. "It's clear on the RTA schedule for that long, nobody signed up for the more inaccessible locations. And the first ones who do, Hetty can fly in aboard the plane, now that the ice is pretty well broken up on the lakes."

Spence grimaced, but only inwardly. He had a couple of backcountry trips booked, and he'd hoped to use the chopper for at least one of them. But his father and uncle so rarely asked for anything for themselves, he wasn't about to put a damper on this.

"So, can I safely presume you don't want to just jump over to Robe Lake?" he asked teasingly, referring to the closest to town and therefore most popular lake.

"Along with every summer tourist arriving in the next month? No, thanks," Dad said.

"Figured," Spence said with a crooked smile to tell his father he'd only been joking.

He walked over to the big map on the back wall of the office. He studied it for a moment, eliminating the most popular places and the places he knew they had already been, although he doubted he knew them all. Alaska was simply too big to know everything. Shelby alone was close to eight national parks and wildlife preserves, plus had about twenty tidewater glaciers that ended at Prince William Sound, the highest concentration in the world.

Someone had once said Alaska was forged by fire but ruled by ice, and Spence thought that was a good description. It was huge, vast, magnificent, forbidding, and often deadly. Visit But Don't Stay was Spence's motto when it came to their clients, who had no idea of just how dangerous this place he loved could be. This place with fifty active volcanoes, two of which usually blew up every year. This place bigger than the next three largest states combined, yet with only five thousand miles of paved road, a thousand less then New York City alone. No, it took a certain kind of spirit and heart to call this wild place home.

Finally, he reached up and tapped a spot on the map.

"How about Tazlina Lake? If you can dodge all the rafters who want to tackle the river, there are a couple of good fishing spots. Especially at the north end. Weather can still be iffy up there this early in the season, so you'd have to pay attention to that, but I'd bet there'd be nobody else to bother you."

"Sounds good to me," Uncle Will said.

Spence opened his mouth to warn them that they'd be heading into higher country, and that while there might not be many two-legged visitors, some of the four-legged inhabitants could get interesting. He shut it again, knowing they both knew that perfectly well and would appropriately prepare.

"Good call," Dad said, his smile telling Spence he'd known exactly what he'd been about to say. "We may have sort of retired, but we haven't forgotten a thing about living in Alaska."

"I pity the bear or moose that tries to take you two on," Spence said and all three of them laughed. "So, when's this expedition taking place?"

"Assuming no shift in the weather pattern, we'll be off in the morning."

"Enjoy," Spence said. Then, a little warily, he asked, "Do I need to check in on Mom and Aunt Sasha while you're gone?"

"I believe they're planning to enjoy this as much as Dad and Uncle Ryan." The words came from behind them as his cousin Parker entered the room.

Spence laughed at that. Parker was probably right. The two women were very close. They had no shortage of things to talk about in that way women did, which seemed never-ending to him.

Parker shoved back his longish, shaggy, dark brown hair. He'd skipped the morning shave again, and Spence knew his always clean-shaven uncle had finally resigned himself to the fact that the stubble was likely going to be a permanent feature.

"You're back early," Spence said.

"It was an easy trip, and my people were quick to settle in at the fishing camp. I'll go back and get them in three days."

Although they specialized in the more remote trips, RTA didn't turn their nose up at more local jaunts if requested. The customer was the one spending the money, after all.

"Nice milk run," Spence said with a grin.

"Yeah, yeah," Parker growled it out in mock irritation. "But I'll take that over your next one."

Spence rolled his eyes. His next scheduled trip was to a remote lakeside fishing spot most easily accessible by floatplane. Which meant more time with Hetty, although that wasn't why he rolled his eyes. He did that because it was a honeymoon trip. He'd made a few of those before and they'd always been a little too…gooey for his taste. All that lovey-dovey stuff seemed a bit over the top to him.

Dealing with it in the closed-in space of the plane cockpit with Hetty was something he didn't want to think about.

"Hetty's pretty excited about getting back into the air again," Parker said.

"Yeah," Spence said noncommittally. Going for a quick subject change, he asked his cousin, "You have all the supplies lined up?"

They were going to restock the permanent campsite they had set up at the lake, which had gotten a lot of use last year. He'd already checked the big, sturdy, wood-framed tent they used for that location, one that fit neatly onto the permanent foundation they'd built so it was a bit more solid than one that just sat on the ground. The still chilly ground.

"It's all ready and waiting in the storage building," Parker said, nodding toward the outbuilding that sat about fifty yards from the main office building they were in now.

"Good. I want to get it loaded on my truck, so I can get it aboard the plane early."

Parker grinned at him. "You just don't want to hang around the newlyweds any longer than you have to."

"Yeah, yeah," Spence muttered, not looking at his cousin.

Later, as he headed out to the storage building to gauge how many trips it would take him to get everything to the dock where the floatplane would tie up, he thought about how true Parker's jab was. He really wasn't looking forward to that aspect of this trip.

And you are not going to waste time analyzing why.

Order to himself given, he pulled open the big sliding door and made himself focus on the task at hand. Parker hadn't lied, it was all here, neatly stacked. The restock supplies, plus the state-required equipment for any flight, food for each person for a week, signaling devices, fishing tackle, an ax/saw combo, fire starter, mosquito nets—the old jokes about bush planes being taken down by a squadron of mosquitos seemed a lot more believable when you spent some time fighting off the huge Alaskan variety—and personal locator beacons.

True, he'd have to figure out what order to put it in the plane's cargo space, and track the weight for load capacity purposes, but he was used to that. Numbers were no problem for him.

He picked up the clipboard that sat atop the stack of boxes and crates and saw the individual weights already listed next to each item, in his cousin Lakin's careful hand. He silently thanked her. That would make up for any extra time he had to spend making sure he was reading the item description right.

And not for the first time, he was thankful for this place, this work, and most of all, this family of his.

Chapter 3

"**W**ant some help?"

Spence looked up to see his sister Kansas standing in the doorway. She wasn't in uniform today, although her long, dark hair was pulled back as usual. She said it was because it got in her way when she was working. Kansas was a state trooper assigned to the search and rescue unit, and if there truly were jobs some people were born to do, his sister had been born for that one.

"Shouldn't you be out rescuing someone?" he teased.

"I am. You," she shot back. Spence laughed. Kansas smiled and shrugged. "Seems everyone's being careful out there today."

"First time for everything," he said wryly.

She pitched right in and they began shifting boxes and crates. He was not at all surprised at how much Kansas could lift. He knew well enough how strong his little sister was. He thought the "little" part but didn't say it, because it irritated her—*Two years isn't that much difference,* she would say—and she was helping him out, after all.

He was mentally gauging the space left in his truck, comparing it to what was left on the inventory list, and deciding which crate to move next when he heard a notification tone unfamiliar to him. He knew from the way Kansas stopped dead and yanked her phone out of her pocket that it was probably something official. He wondered if it was a call-out, if somebody out there had stopped being careful, or if Alaska had decided to teach some puny human a needed lesson about life in the wild.

Kansas swiped the screen, read what was there, smiled, tapped out a couple of quick sentences, sent the message, and put the phone back in her pocket.

"No emergency?" he asked.

"No. Just a text from Scott Montgomery, a guy who works with Eli. A forensics guy. He looked up something on an old case for me."

"An old case?"

"Yeah. That kid we found last year, out in the Kenai Wildlife Refuge."

"I remember that. The kid you found with that herd of…what were they? The ones that look like mountain goats only with killer horns?"

"Dall sheep. I'd never seen one up close before. It was funny, how they almost seemed to be protecting him. Like they knew he was young and harmless to them. Anyway, I wanted contact info, to see how the kid's doing, and Scott just happened to answer the phone. He was nice about it, like he always is, and looked it up for me."

That was very Kansas, following up on something she was hardly required to. She was nothing if not passionate about her work, as he knew from the times a search ended badly. She took it hard, was occasionally even distraught at what she saw as failure. And he'd heard she had no qualms about unleashing her anger on people she didn't feel were as dedicated to the work as she was. The Coltons were not a retiring bunch.

She was coming back from the truck for another box when she unexpectedly said, "You ever wonder what we'd be doing if Mom and Dad had never left San Diego?"

"Nah," he said. "All that heat, concrete, asphalt, traffic?" He gave an exaggerated shudder. "Too scary."

She laughed. But then her tone changed to very serious. "You really love it here, don't you."

It wasn't really a question, more of an observation. Of the obvious, he thought, but he answered her anyway. "I do. I would not want to live anywhere else."

"Neither would I," she said quietly. "And not because of what happened down there."

Spence stopped, shutting down the jokes, sensing his sister was in a serious mood at the moment. He put down the crate he'd started to lift and turned to face her.

"You okay? What brought this on?"

"I talked to Eli this morning. He had a question about one of our rescue cases from a few months ago. Which was what made me think of the Kenai kid. Anyway, he sounded kind of…something. I asked what was wrong, and he just said it was the date." She grimaced. "It took me a while and a calendar check to understand. It's…or it would have been, Aunt Caroline's birthday tomorrow."

Spence grimaced. "Damn."

He knew the family story, of course, but it wasn't in-grained in him, or Kansas, to the point where the date would have even occurred to them. When he'd gotten old enough to understand tragedy and trauma a little better, he'd tried to imagine how Eli must've felt. Spence had never known Caroline, but Eli had. What would it have felt like to be there when the body was found?

She'd been beautiful; he'd seen the pictures. A rising star in the modeling world at a young age, still in high school, she had attracted many fans. One of them in particular was mentally unstable and vicious. That twisted, sick fan had come to the house to kidnap Caroline. Instead, he had brutally murdered the grandparents Spence had never known, Edward and Mia Colton. He hadn't stopped there, continuing with the apparently unplanned murder of Caroline herself. The killer had then arranged himself with Caroline on the living room sofa and taken his own life. When Uncle Will and Eli had arrived, it had taken them a moment to realize they were both dead. And then they'd found her parents, slaughtered upstairs.

Spence couldn't imagine ever being able to put that out of your mind.

To him and Kansas, it was history, but Eli had lived it. At five years old, he had been old enough to have the ugly scenes and the trauma etched into his memory. Spence had always figured it was why Eli had chosen the career path he had.

It had also been big news, in all the headlines, and he knew the day Uncle Will had found the media camped out in front of Eli's school had been the day the decision had been made. And three months later, the Coltons were in Alaska, far from the chaos of Southern California.

"I'm glad we didn't have to live through all that," Kansas said. "Although I think we might understand it all better if we had."

"Maybe. What I try to focus on is afterward. That, together, Uncle Will and Dad built this, and because of that I'm able to do what I love."

"And I found the one thing in life that I was meant to do," Kansas agreed. "Maybe…maybe because it's that day, we should say something."

Spence's brow furrowed. "Say something?"

"To Dad and Uncle Will. About how glad we are they did what they did, and how sorry we are that they had to go through…that. That we know the life we have now is because they got through it."

That was so like Kansas. When she cared about something, she went full bore. Not that that made him any more comfortable with the idea of getting all sappy and emotional with everybody. But maybe she did have a point. Maybe it did deserve acknowledgment, at least.

"I don't want to make a huge deal out of it," he said, "but I see your point."

"I don't think they'd want a huge deal, either. I know Eli didn't, because I tried and he changed the subject so fast it was dizzying. But I still think they need to know that we know. That just because we were born after it all happened doesn't mean we don't know and care about the hell it must have been."

For a long silent moment, Spence just stared at her. And then, because it was the only thing he could think of to do, he crossed the three feet between them and hugged her.

"You're really something, little sister."

"You're not so bad yourself. For an annoying big brother, that is."

He laughed. "Well, if you're going to say something to

them, do it now because both Dad and Uncle Will are head-ing out tomorrow…"

His words trailed off as something that should have been obvious hit him. No wonder the two men wanted out of town tomorrow. And that decided him. Kansas was right. He should at least acknowledge what had happened even if he'd never known their sister, the woman who would have been his aunt. He wanted them to know he understood.

"Thanks, sis," he murmured and hugged her again.

She was right. His family had always been there for him, so he could—and would—do no less in return.

Chapter 4

Hetty stifled an early morning yawn as she read the email Parker had forwarded to her last night before she headed downstairs from her apartment to her car. It was from a client whose family she'd flown down to Kodiak Island, raving about what a great time they'd had. And while it was mostly about their guide, which of course had been Spence, there were some very kind words about their pilot as well. Her.

The note made her smile and she sent a quick thanks back to Parker. He was pretty good about that. She doubted he realized how she and Spence grated on each other sometimes—or at least how Spence grated on her, since Spence didn't seem to show much of anything behind that jovial exterior—but he took care to send them all the responses like this one. And despite everything, when it came to their jobs, she and Spence always did their best. If she did say so, their best was pretty darn good.

Even if too many of the rave reviews from female clients were mostly gushing praise of her partner.

It doesn't matter, she told herself.

And it didn't, really. It didn't matter if every client gushed over him, or flirted with him. Or if he flirted back.

It mattered nothing at all, to her anyway. She just did her job, and darn well. To be honest, so did he. He just had more one-on-one time with the clients, and so it was only natural there would be more of a…relationship. Of sorts.

Besides, it was quite obvious Spence only flirted with those he found attractive—who else?—and they were all coquettish and a bit shallow-seeming to her. So, obviously, that's what appealed to him. While she herself was businesslike, levelheaded, and maybe a bit brusque. So it was clear that, if the kind of women he flirted with were what he wanted, he'd certainly want nothing at all to do with her. Not in that way, anyway. Which was just as well. That was a company pool she did not want to swim in. Especially with him.

At least she knew, because he was a Colton and they couldn't care less, it had nothing to do with her being biracial. Her mother, the contributor of her darker skin, had sat her down when she'd become a teenager and explained that there were those it would matter to. It had been her beloved late father—he of the green eyes—who had told her bluntly to tell them to get lost. His anger at the very idea of someone insulting his daughter had warmed her heart, as he so often had. And he had also greatly respected the Coltons, and she knew he would have been pleased when she'd gone to work for RTA.

But that didn't mean he would have wanted her dating one of them. That she didn't swim in the dating pool at all, with anyone, was another matter. She simply didn't have the time.

She repeated the oft-used—most often with her mother—excuse to herself. It wasn't just an excuse, it was the truth. What little spare time she had she preferred to spend in the quiet solitude of her own living room, reading, catching a movie or keeping up on developments in the flying world. Maybe it was an overreaction to growing up in a big family, or maybe she simply liked the peace.

Already weary of these unusual thoughts that had caught hold of her this morning, she made herself focus on today. She grabbed up her small backpack, the one she took on every trip just in case, filled with extra clothes and toiletries. They had a lot of gear already in the plane, but she just felt better if she had this with her. Hers was nothing compared to Spence's though, which was three times the size; a fact she never failed to rag on him about. She didn't know what all he lugged around in the thing, beyond a first-aid kit and the RTA radio for the times when they were out of cell phone range, which was often.

He was the one who also went armed, which thankfully saved her from having to do it. The state law requiring pilots to be armed had been changed after 9/11, but no one who knew anything ventured into the Alaskan wilds without protection of some kind. And for them, that fell to Spence, who happened to be an excellent shot with that rifle of his. True, he didn't carry it every minute, but it was always fairly close by. She appreciated that, and that he did it without comment, except for joking he didn't care if he could hit a pine cone at a thousand yards with it. He cared if he could carry it on a twenty-mile hike, climb and still stop a berserk moose if he had to.

Hetty knew how to shoot, she understood the necessity, but hitting a living target was something else altogether. She wasn't sure she could shoot an animal regardless of the situation. She didn't begrudge those who did, it was a huge part of Alaskan culture, but it wasn't for her.

At least she didn't have to have her usual battle on the usual topic with herself before a trip with Spence. Half the time she wanted to call in sick when she knew she was going to be partnered with him for an excursion. For all her rationalization, watching him flirt rubbed her the wrong way and she had to work to hide her reaction to it. It was a distraction, and she did not want distractions when up in the air. For all the joy she got from flying, she took her work very seriously.

But today's flight was a honeymoon couple and the bride would—she assumed—be so wrapped up in her new husband she'd barely notice their handsome, sexy guide.

I wonder if Spence will feel slighted?

As soon as she thought it, she quashed the idea. For all his nearly provocative come-ons, it only happened when the interest was obviously mutual. He never made the first move—well, in words anyway, it never went beyond that, that she knew of—and if the other party didn't start, he remained as businesslike as she herself did.

And she had to give him credit…he was always so good with the shy ones. Adults or kids, Spence worked to draw them out as much as he could, to make sure they enjoyed their venture into this land he so loved.

Yes, there was much to like about Spence Colton, and if the irritations sometimes outweighed that to her, that was her problem, not his. He was who he was, he'd overcome problems that sidelined many in life—and who knew that better than her?—and if he chose to use his other assets a bit up front, then who was she to judge?

That settled, she headed for the door. She went down the stairs quietly, care she always took so as not to disturb whoever might be in the usually hushed art studio downstairs from her small apartment. The owner of the building had given her a break on the rent because of the need to be quiet, but since it was her nature anyway, she would have stayed without the perk. It was enough of a novelty to be away from her big, sometimes chaotic, family.

Of course, she was now working for a big, sometimes chaotic, family. And even if she wasn't, she'd be spending time with them anyway because her family had always been close with all the Coltons. In the case of her younger brother Troy, very close; he'd been dating Lakin Colton since he was fifteen.

She smothered an inward sigh. Her little brother had his personal life pretty much in order, while she still drifted. Not that she hadn't ever dated, she had, and once it had been serious. Or so she'd thought. But when she'd realized the man in question had city life in mind, preferably someplace big and highly populated, she'd known it would never work. She didn't mind a visit now and then, but after that, coming home always felt like escaping.

Spence never left this wild place at all, if he could help it.

And there she was, thinking about her annoying partner again. And no matter how often she told herself it was natural to think about the guy you worked with so closely so often, it didn't seem to help much. It was still maddening that she couldn't keep her thoughts from veering in his direction, most times with no warning whatsoever. Her normally quick, decisive mind always slipped the leash where he was concerned.

By the time Hetty got to the RTA headquarters, she thought she had herself well under control. She would focus on this trip and nothing else. And if watching a newlywed, happy couple together ate at her, she would keep it hidden. Well hidden. She didn't need that as part of her life.

But did she want that...a husband? A family of her own?

She sighed inwardly as she got out of her car and walked toward the familiar building with the A-frame roof over the entry. She was one of seven kids, so family was part and parcel of who and what she was, as was the devastating loss of her father. That was still an ache, even several years later. But she also savored the peace and quiet of her apartment alone, away from all of her family's well-meaning machinations. She wasn't quite sure she wanted to follow the path her parents had, producing kid after kid. Besides, if she was pregnant, she'd have to stop flying, at least for a while, and she didn't like that idea. At all.

The absurdity of worrying about the impact having children might have on her life while at the same time avoiding any serious dating struck her, and she was practically laughing at herself by the time she went through the door.

"Did I miss the joke?"

She managed not to stop dead when she heard Spence's voice the moment the door closed behind her.

She didn't turn to look at him. "You often do," she said, making sure her voice was so cheerful that no one else in the room—Parker and Lakin were both there—would take it as a jab.

"Oh, he's not that bad," Lakin said teasingly, defending her cousin.

"Ha," said Parker, leaving Spence nothing to do but take it as a joke.

"Yeah, yeah," he muttered. He looked at his cousin. "The big bosses get off okay this morning?"

Parker nodded. "Left right on schedule."

"Of course," Lakin added, grinning. The senior Coltons were nothing if not efficient.

"So," Spence said to Parker, "what's the big news?"

Hetty, having just set her backpack down on one of the chairs in the lobby area, turned to look at Parker, curious. Big news?

"Well, let's just say your day suddenly got freed up."

Spence frowned. "What?"

Lakin sighed audibly. "The Greshams canceled."

Hetty drew back in surprise. "Just now?"

Parker nodded. "Seems Mr. Gresham took ill last night. Must be serious, if they're willing to take the cancellation hit."

Hetty knew there was a percentage fee for cancellations within twenty-four hours before an excursion was scheduled to begin. Perhaps oddly, she was disappointed. She liked this particular flight to her favorite lake. And besides, she'd been waiting excitedly to get back in the air now that the ice on the sound and most of the nearby lakes had finally broken.

"Well, that leaves a gaping hole in my weekend," Spence grumbled, sounding as if he was as disappointed as she was. And he probably was. For all her frustration with him, she'd never denied that Spence loved this work as much as she did. His passion for the land and its inhabitants rang through in his voice whenever he spoke to their guests.

She thought quickly and then looked at Parker. "I want to take the plane up anyway, make sure everything checks out. I can do a circuit, check the usual sites and fishing camps, see how everything looks before we get really deep into the season."

"Not a bad idea," Parker agreed. He looked at Spence. "You need to do the restock of this destination site anyway, right?"

Rats. She'd forgotten that one of the tasks at hand had been to resupply the campsite they'd been headed to.

"Yes," Spence said.

"You don't have to go this time," Hetty said quickly. "The next excursion up there isn't until a couple of weeks from now, right?"

Spence shifted his gaze to her, and those blue eyes felt even more intense than usual. "I've already got the plane loaded up. It would be silly not to just get it done now."

She had no argument. She should have checked the plane first, before she'd come here to the office, then she would have known and wouldn't have embarrassed herself trying to talk him out of going with her on this first flight of the season.

"Oh," she said rather lamely.

"You two go get that done, then we'll be ready to go for the Radfords in a couple of weeks," Parker said. He added, with a grin, "Then we'll be back to all aircraft assigned and out, and Lakin and I can take the day off."

She knew that was about as likely as...nothing.

"And we've got another reservation for next week, for the Soundview site," Lakin put in. "After that, we're booked

pretty solid for the rest of the summer. You two are going
to be working hard this year."

And the brother and sister who essentially ran this place
most of the time turned and walked back to their offices,
unaware of the kick in the head they'd just delivered to
their chief pilot.

Chapter 5

"Hey, where's your passengers?"

Spence looked at Jake, the teenager who worked part-time maintaining the docking facilities. "They canceled, last minute."

Jake frowned. "Oh. There was someone down looking at the plane, I thought it was your guy. Must have just been a tourist."

"'Tis the season,'" Spence said. He glanced at Hetty, who wasn't looking at either of them. "We're going to make the trip anyway, to drop off the new season supplies, since I've already got them loaded up. Thanks again for the help with that, by the way."

The boy grinned. "Thanks for the freebie at The Cove. It'll smooth things over with my girl."

Spence grinned. "Bring her some flowers, too. My mom said they just got a delivery in at the market in town."

"Good idea," Jake said.

The kid walked away, whistling happily. Spence smiled to himself. He wasn't going to use that gift certificate a client had tipped him with anyway, so it might as well go to a good cause, smoothing over a tiff between young lovers.

"You gave him that certificate for a free dinner and dessert Mrs. Barnes gave you?"

He turned to find Hetty looking at him quizzically. He shrugged. "I wasn't going to use it. Somebody might as well."

"Why not?"

"Exactly."

She blinked, figured it out and grimaced at him. "I meant why weren't you going to use it?"

He shrugged. "I just wasn't."

He didn't really want to discuss his love life—or decided lack thereof lately—with Hetty of all people. It had become almost a chore to keep up the lighthearted, flirty exterior in front of her. But he felt like he had to. It was a barrier of sorts between them and he needed it to be there. Why, he didn't want to delve into, now or ever.

"Nice of you, then," she said.

"It happens, despite what you think," he said and immediately regretted the jab.

"I've never disputed that you can be a nice guy, when you want to be. When you're not being—"

She cut herself off so sharply he was sure he knew what she'd been about to say. She had said it, more than once. *When you're not being a shameless flirt.*

She'd been saying it since high school, when that flirting and his looks had been all it had taken to charm almost anyone on campus. Anyone female, that is. Well, except Hetty, who had apparently been immune then and clearly still was.

It had taken his prowess on a baseball diamond or his skill on skates and with a hockey stick to impress the guys. And his willingness to take a hit, if it would help the team.

That was something he'd learned early on. Because his family—which to him meant all the Coltons, not just his own parents and sister, but Uncle Will and Aunt Sasha and his four cousins, too—was a team. A team with an unbreakable bond, who all pulled together under any circumstances. Because they'd paid the highest price once, for not doing just that.

And the aunt he'd never known, Caroline, had paid with her life for the lack of that bond back then.

Believe.

It was the Colton family motto now. If you had a problem or were in trouble, the one thing you could be sure of was that the family would believe you. Because, long ago, they hadn't.

Spence gave a sharp shake of his head, wondering why his mind was wandering off like that. Maybe to avoid having to deal with Hetty. If so, it had worked, because she'd walked away to do her safety check before they took off.

He checked his backpack of what he considered standard gear—never mind that Hetty teased him mercilessly about the size of it—one final time. His Kimber Mountain Ascent was strapped to one side. He knew some folks didn't agree with his decision to carry the very lightweight rifle, which was under five pounds without any added gear like his scope. And if he was out here to hunt big game, he'd agree and carry something heavier. But he didn't carry it for that. It was for protection, and all he cared about in that mode was that the bullet went where he aimed it. He wasn't out to be a sniper, he just wanted that bear or ticked-off moose to decide he had better things to do than go after a piddly little human.

He also checked his Blackfoot knife in its sheath attached to his belt before he slung the backpack over his shoulder. Since Hetty's pack was also right there on the dock, he picked it up, too, and lugged them both into the plane and stowed them carefully in the racks just behind the cockpit. He stood there for a moment, staring at the copilot seat.

On flights like this, he was usually back in the passenger area, talking to the clients, explaining a few specific things about their destination if they were old hands, explaining a lot more if they were newbies. But today there would be no one and no reason for him to be back there. No reason for him not to sit up front. Except one.

Spence felt suddenly as if a battle was raging inside him. His brain was saying, *Of course, sit in front. It would be silly not to.* Besides, he liked it up front, where he could look out over this place that stirred him like no other, where he could spot the locations he'd been to fish or hike or just breathe in that Alaskan air.

Not to mention his other favorite view, which was her.

But his gut was saying, *Stay back there, as far away as you can get.* Because it would be torture. And Hetty wouldn't want him up front anyway. Or would she? Whenever they had clients who wanted to sit up front, or who wanted their kid to, she'd never seemed to mind, and even found things for them to do. But that was a paying client. Not her RTA partner she could barely stand to be around.

He could ask, he supposed.

Now there's a concept. Just ask.

He could almost hear his cousin Mitchell, the ever-practical lawyer, the one who cleaned up messes for all the Coltons, saying the words with a roll of his eyes.

He went back down the steps to the dock. Hetty was just finishing up her exterior check. She glanced at him then went back to making a note in the small notebook she carried. Old school, perhaps, but necessary here. It always came as a shock to some of their guests that there were actually places where WiFi didn't exist and you were actually offline the entire time you were there. They had it at the headquarters building, courtesy of a satellite link, but out at the camp, there was nary a cell tower nor an internet connection in sight. And he kind of liked it that way.

"We need to top off the avgas?" he asked, thinking about the necessary fuel for the flight.

She shook her head. "We're good. We'll be flying light, even with the cargo load, without the two intended passengers and their gear."

He nodded in acknowledgment, hesitated, then said it. "You mind if I sit up front, or would you prefer me out of your way?"

She went still, her hand stopping midnotation. It was a moment before she looked at him and he wondered, rather urgently, what she was thinking.

But all she said was, "Your choice."

He didn't know whether to be pleased or disappointed that she hadn't made the decision for him. At least she hadn't said, "Stay out of my way."

Up front it was then. He'd just sit, keep his mouth shut and enjoy the view. He'd go through it in his mind, thinking about how each place was on foot. As they passed over the east end of Chugach State Park, he'd ponder his last hike at Columbia Peak. Then the lakes. He'd always loved the symmetry of them, all of similar shape, crescents that were laid out in order of size from the smallest Tonsina to the largest, Tazlina.

He had the thought he should tell Hetty not to buzz too low at Tazlina, or his dad and uncle might think they were searching for them. He turned to look at her, but the words died in his throat.

Hetty Amos made that plain, RTA shirt look…well, sexy. He couldn't tell if she was wearing makeup, but if she was she was doing it right, because, well, he couldn't tell. All he knew was she looked amazing.

He turned back to looking out the window. He'd best just sit here and enjoy that view.

And avoid the other view he loved.

Would you prefer me out of your way?

Yes! She'd wanted to say it. She'd wanted to shout it. But she already knew, in her gut, that having him out of sight did not equal having him out of mind. So if he was going to be in her thoughts anyway, he might as well sit up where he could see better. She knew how much he loved watching the landscape unroll before them, and she wasn't cold enough to deprive anyone of that.

Besides, of all the fishing camps they flew to, this one was the closest, so it wasn't going to be a long flight anyway. Which was probably just as well. She was already twitchy.

She walked to the end of the dock and looked out toward the sound. While it wasn't rough, it wasn't anywhere near glassy smooth, either. Which was good, since she hated dealing with the excess surface tension of glassy water. She would have liked a little more wind to head into for the takeoff, but this would do. At least once they taxied out of the marina there would be all the room the Cessna needed to take off. Unknowing passengers were sometimes surprised at how much room a seaplane needed to take off because of the hydrodynamic drag of the floats.

No, it should be a normal takeoff; one she'd done hundreds of times. But there was no plane less forgiving of sloppy piloting than a seaplane, so she knew better than to take anything for granted.

She did a final check of the cargo, although she knew Spence was always careful. He might not be a pilot, but he understood the center-of-gravity concept, and how important it was in flying floatplanes.

He also knew enough to help Jake push them off from the dock and then quickly make the jump aboard before she turned on the engine. A floatplane under power was moving, whether you wanted it to or not.

Spence chose the front seat, as she'd expected. At least he turned off auto-flirt when it was just them. And she knew he knew the basics of the instruments and controls, just in case.

She lowered the water rudders and upped the power to the engine until they were taxiing away from the RTA dock at a pace she was comfortable with. For some reason, a memory came back to her from a picnic-style gathering of RTA people the owners had hosted. She been the newest hire at the time, and as always, was grateful they'd taken a chance on her, a relatively inexperienced pilot. She'd been afraid she'd have to leave Alaska to get that first job. When she'd said as much, Ryan Colton, Spence's dad, had smiled at her and said, "We like when we can hire people we already know and trust."

"Too bad you can't handle a boat, too," one of their crew had joked. "I could use a break now and then."

"The heck she can't." Spence had jumped in. "That plane's a boat until it's airborne."

She'd wanted to hug him, and might have if there hadn't been so many people there, including all of his family. That was the Spence she remembered, the boy with more discernment than anyone gave him credit for. Looking back now, she thought it was probably the moment when her high school crush on Spence Colton had reactivated. And refused to die, even when she watched him flirt with clients, because she knew, she just knew, there was more to him.

She even had proof, like the time they'd been prepping to take the Alexander family out to the main fishing camp. The parents had been worried the kids would get bored with no internet, so he'd talked to them a bit and found out they liked this one board game even if it was hopelessly old school. So, Spence had gone out and tracked down an edition of the game in a secondhand store and packed it up with the rest of the gear. When she'd realized what he'd done, she'd practically melted inside. That was the Spence she knew lived beneath the casual, carefree exterior. The Spence she remembered from the hours they'd spent together fighting through his quirky way of learning.

The Spence she'd never forgotten, for so many reasons. Even if the man sitting beside her now seemed like a surface imitation.

The takeoff was uneventful, as she'd hoped. Their destination, when they got there, would be a different matter. Partially because the lake was so much smaller and she'd have to taxi them out from the campsite to where she could utilize more of its length for takeoff. But it was also usually a bit windier there, which would help with faster liftoff.

She chuckled inwardly at herself. *Get there first, before you worry about leaving.*

"Something funny?" Spence asked, sounding wary.

"Just me getting ahead of myself," she said.

"You always think ahead. It's a requirement, isn't it, to be as good as you are?"

Yes, that was one thing about Spence she could always count on. He never failed to compliment her on her flying. He might joke about everything else, might be a goofball sometimes about some things, but not about this.

"I do try to think ahead," she agreed. "And thanks."

He shrugged. "Truth is truth."

Yes, it was. And the truth was the same as it had always been since the first time she'd laid eyes on Spence Colton and had felt a totally unexpected jolt of attraction. And that she knew she could never, ever have him, didn't ease that feeling one bit.

Chapter 6

Spence wondered if the jolt of adrenaline he always felt when they took off was even a tenth of what she felt. One sideways glance at Hetty, at the sheer glow of exuberance, made him doubt it. Then again, when he looked out over the landscape below them as they banked and turned from the sound toward the mountains, he felt that burst of energy that always followed the knowledge that he was once more headed into the wild. So maybe it was just as powerful as what she felt, only different.

He looked down over the foothills—which would be considered mountains themselves in many places in the world—and saw that even the patches of snow that usually lingered in the shady, sheltered spots were gone. He wondered if he was strange, for being almost sad to see the last of the snow melt away. Maybe it was because they had fewer clients in the dead of winter, and he was more free to go trekking on his own. He knew his family worried when he, or Mitchell, took off alone as they were wont to do, but he was extra careful, always prepared, and then more careful.

This area was fairly close to Shelby and wasn't as wild as some of the places he visited. Especially including those he kept to himself, never taking clients there even though to him they were the most beautiful places he'd ever been. There was nothing like standing looking at a gorgeous, crystalline lake, and only having to turn your head to see an unstoppable glacier creeping down from the peaks. Or having the eagles soaring overhead and sparing barely a glance for the insignificant human below.

He never felt more alive than when he was out in the vastness of it. The wildness was the reason he went to those places, and he didn't want that to change. Didn't want them on the list of places RTA took people. Selfish, perhaps, but there were some things he just wanted to keep to himself.

As he scanned the horizon ahead and on both sides, he felt the urge to go higher, so he could see more. Almost in the same instant, he felt the shift, the climb, and knew that she was already doing it. He turned his head to grin at them being in sync, just as she said, loudly enough to be heard over the noise since he hadn't put on the plane's headphones yet, "I just want to check the status of the main spots."

He nodded and belatedly reached for the headphones, activated them and slipped them on.

"Just what I was going to suggest," he said. "Last year the north camp didn't become accessible until the beginning of August. Need to know that before we start booking anything there."

She bobbed her head. They banked smoothly into a turn, and since she was intent on the maneuver, he felt free to watch her. It was so clear in her face, in her eyes, that she loved what she was doing, it might as well have been written in neon above her head. She loved flying as much as he loved exploring this place where he'd been lucky enough to be born.

He tried to remember, back in the days when it had just been the two of them in a classroom as she'd tried to help him figure out what seemed to come so easily to other kids, if she'd talked about learning to fly. He couldn't remember that she had, but he'd been so focused on his own frustrations that he might not have noticed. He'd had a few appointments with people who could supposedly help him with his reading issues. None had. He knew his parents had been worried, so his mask of it not mattering to him got thicker, even with them. He'd hidden his problem from his friends for so long, feeling ashamed, they thought the times when he made some mistake were intentional, all part of that joking façade.

But because Hetty was practically family, and had volunteered to tutor him through a school mentoring program—and because he knew her well enough to know she would never use it against him—he had finally let it out.

And to his amazement, once he had explained, she'd made it her mission to find a way to help him. And she had never lost her temper with him, had never chastised him or gotten irritated or thrown in the towel. Never thought he was stupid, just different. And she ever and always ended a session with, "We'll try again."

And it had been Hetty who had come up with the idea that had finally worked, so that he was able to function almost normally in a written-word-driven world. And he would never forget that. He trusted her more than any person who wasn't blood family, and all her teasing and jabbing couldn't change that.

Too bad telling himself that's all he felt for her wasn't working so well.

Soon they were circling over the small high-country clearing that got less interest than the fishing camps, but got a lot from people looking for isolation, a respite from the madness of the everyday world. He understood that. It was sort of what he was sad to see go when summer and the high-traffic tourist season rolled around. Although he tended to like better those who had never been here before who came wanting to see the more remote places. He'd always figured they had something in common under the surface, more so than he had with those who just came looking for the best fishing spot.

But that season was what allowed him to live the way he wanted, so he wasn't about to complain. RTA was supporting his preferred lifestyle and keeping his cousins Parker and Lakin busy as well. Not to mention all the other people they employed.

Including the woman beside him, handling the controls of the Cessna with such calm competence. And who much preferred this season for flying. She'd told him once that with the stark, unbroken ice white of winter, it was too easy for pilots to lose the sense of how high—or low—they really were. And she didn't like the retractable skis for snow landings, or the extra bounce. Give her a smooth water landing any time.

Her long, dark hair was pulled back as usual, he guessed in part so it didn't get in the way of the headphones. He'd asked her once if the noise canceling didn't impair her ability to hear a potential problem with the engine, and she'd explained that it helped instead, by toning down the constant steady drone, so that anything unusual in fact actually stood out more.

He yanked his focus away from her and shifted position so he could look down below.

"That quaking aspen went down," he murmured to himself, making a mental note. He'd noticed the last time he was up there that the thirty-foot tree was leaning rather precariously. He'd taken a close look and seen no sign of damage or infestation, but there had been a large root making its way from a neighboring spruce and he'd suspected that was what was tilting the much smaller aspen. He'd need to come up here with some equipment and cut into logs, then split, since it didn't dry well in the round. The wood wasn't something he'd want for lots of heat or length of burn, but it was great to get things started, especially for people who might not be expert fire builders.

"Good excuse to get up here, huh?"

Hetty's voice in his ears told him he'd muttered that louder than he'd thought he had. But he didn't deny it. Just looked at her and grinned as he said, "Yep."

"Learn to skydive and I'll drop you off," she quipped.

His grin widened. He liked this Hetty, relaxed and willing to joke. Usually quite brisk and businesslike around clients, she would never kid around.

"My luck, I'd land on the chainsaw I need to bring."

She laughed before saying, "You have what you need?"

Not really.

His gut knotted at his own thought. Because what he needed was this Hetty, lighthearted and at ease. And he needed her a lot more than he wanted to admit.

"Yeah," he said, his voice a little rough as he fought

down his unwanted response to her cheerful mood. "Everything else looks good."

She nodded and banked the plane to turn toward their next flyover, the fishing camp RTA had built a few years ago, which had become one of their most popular. As he usually did coming out of that turn, he remembered the flight when a thick cloud layer had dropped in, masking the mountains around them. Then the wind below it had kicked up and they'd been a bit tossed. Staying under the clouds but not being trapped in a valley between mountains without room to turn around, or any place to land, had been the real trick. Hetty hadn't turned a hair and handled it as if it were any routine flight. Because that's what she did.

But today was clear and he had a great view. He could see nothing from the air that indicated any problems, so he checked the camp off his mental list.

And finally they were done with the airborne survey and headed for their destination. He glanced at his watch. After noon, but they'd still have time for him to get all the gear, food and other supplies off-loaded, and the tent he jokingly called a "canvas house" put in place for the next excursion. The Radford family were regulars and he knew they'd never missed a trip once it was set.

It wasn't long—or didn't seem that way because of his mood, which was in turn because of Hetty's mood—before he spotted the gleam of the sun on the lake up ahead. They circled above first, so he could take a look at the area surrounding the cleared campsite. He didn't see anything amiss and was about to give the okay to take them on in when he heard an odd, high-pitched sound he didn't recognize. He looked at Hetty and realized she'd changed. Gone was the relaxed, easygoing woman of a few moments ago. In her place was a taut, focused pilot.

"That squeal?" he asked.

She didn't answer, only nodded again, clearly focused on all her instruments and the controls.

He remembered her once saying the plane talked to you, if you knew how to listen. A change in pitch, the variance between engine noise and airframe noise, it all meant different things. She'd explained, in almost professorial tones, how hearing was second only to vision in maintaining awareness while flying. And that sounds had three variables that all provided data. "Frequency, intensity and duration," she'd quoted at him.

He also remembered asking her if frequency meant the pitch of the sound or how often it happened. She'd given him that now-all-too-rare smile that he'd first seen when he'd begun to make rapid progress back in those tutoring days, when the pieces had started to fall together visually in his mind.

"Both," she'd said approvingly.

He snapped out of the memory, special though it was, to focus on the present. Which, judging by her demeanor, might not be pleasant at all.

He looked up front to see, thankfully, the propeller still spinning normally. Then he shifted his gaze back to her, awaiting any sign or request—no, judging by the set of her jaw, it would be an order—that he do something.

"Fuel's dropping too fast. We're going straight in to landing—" She broke off in the same moment the prop stopped turning.

They were definitely going down.

Chapter 7

Everything she'd ever learned raced through Hetty's mind. She'd been through the drill countless times, her flight instructors shutting the engine off and leaving it to her to get them down safely. She'd done it multiple times, on both land and water. It wasn't as catastrophic as civilians thought it would be—an engine failing. Of course, it was a bit easier when you'd known the instructor beside you would take over if need be.

But still, it wasn't like they were in a helicopter, after all. An airplane without a functioning engine became, in essence, a glider. A not particularly efficient one, true—and the pontoons of a floatplane made it even worse because of all the drag—but a glider nonetheless. A machine designed to fly. Which meant they had time. Not much, but some.

Her mind raced, assessing. They were, or had been, at about five thousand feet. As she had already said to herself, floatplanes didn't have the best glide ratio, but there was currently no headwind to slow them down further. But distance wasn't really the concern, since they were essentially over their destination landing spot.

Minimum descent rate.

She chanted the words as she tried to restart the engine.

No good. She banked slightly as they lost elevation. Tried again. No go. She couldn't figure out what had happened, but time enough for that once they were safely down. Since they were directly over what had been their intended touch-down location anyway, she decided to use the momentum they had left to land safely, with enough left, hopefully, to get them ashore. They had the inflatable kayak on board to use if they had to, but she would prefer not to have to use it.

I'd prefer to have my engine still running!

She gave it a third and last try, with the same result. That decided the issue. She would have to land this ungainly glider without power.

Hetty adjusted her approach heading so that they'd be aimed straight for the small beach that helped make this such a popular spot. There would be no turns after the last visual reference. She'd touch down as close to it as she could and still have room for the drag of the water to slow them enough.

When she was set, when they were committed, she said to Spence, "Call it in. I have a feeling we won't be going back the same way we got here."

She saw him reach for the radio. It was the last thing she saw other than the controls and the water below as they dropped. They were going to hit faster than usual because they'd need the speed to be sure they had enough flare, so she adjusted to make sure the pontoons didn't dig in and flip them. She talked to herself, running through her mental checklist continuously, so focused, she only vaguely heard Spence on the radio talking to RTA.

The touchdown was a jolt, but not that much stronger than usual. The slowdown was immediate, the water dragging them quickly. She adjusted the flaps to maintain as much momentum as possible. When they'd reached a safe enough speed, she dropped the rudders, although she was happy to see she'd judged that about right and they were headed straight for the beach.

She concentrated on keeping the Cessna straight, since she couldn't maneuver with anything but the rudders and what forward motion they still had left.

Hetty thought back to the last time she'd been here. They had been tied up to the small dock then. But she didn't have the option for that kind of finesse this time. She'd walked the beach here regularly, just in case, to see if there were any changes she needed to know about. That precaution paid off now because, unless there had been a new rock-slide in the interim that had sent something big rolling all the way down, the beach was wide enough and smooth enough that this should work.

She spared a split second to be thankful RTA had gone for pontoons tough enough to withstand some grinding, because they were going to hit that beach. She thought it with an inward smile, a combination of pride in the organization she worked for and, to be honest, a little pride in herself for pulling this off rather neatly. They would run out of speed a little short of grounding, but not by much.

She turned her head to tell Spence he was going to have to get a little wet, but he was already moving. A moment later, he was thigh-deep in the ice-cold water, without even a wince. He'd grabbed the tie-off rope and used it to pull the plane the last few feet. And he made it look easy, although she knew that essentially towing even a floatplane was no simple task. Sometimes she forgot just how strong he was, even though she knew. She'd certainly watched him enough times; the way he hefted the big supply crates, the way he climbed when out on a hike, the way he—

Stop it!

She wrote off her sudden veering into forbidden territory to the at-last-ebbing adrenaline. What she needed to be thinking about right now was what had gone wrong, not the very apparent physical prowess of Spence Colton.

Hetty felt the shift when the plane was a land creature once more. She picked up the radio to notify RTA they were safely down, and after the relieved congratulations, got the news she'd expected—with all aircraft out on excursions, they were there until morning.

She shut down everything, clambered out and down to the port pontoon, walking to the front end and hopping off, getting only her boots wet. As opposed to Spence, whose jeans were wet past his knees as he tied the Cessna off to a large, heavy-looking log half buried on the beach. He leaned into it as if to make sure it would hold, then straightened and turned.

As soon as she was on the beach, he ran at her, startling her. He caught her in those strong arms she'd just been admiring and, with an almost wild-sounding laugh, he lifted her up and spun her around.

"You are the best, Cap'n Amos!"

She started to laugh herself but it died in her throat. Died because he'd planted an enthusiastic kiss on her cheek. Because he'd planted a kiss on her cheek and that's not where she wanted him to kiss her.

"We're alive," she managed to get out with difficulty because he was still holding her tightly. "It could have been worse."

"Sure," he said, laughing with what she recognized as an aftereffect of an adrenaline spike. "We could have been in a helicopter."

Despite her nervous state—from his embrace, not the landing—she mastered her usual response. "That's why I fly the machine that wants to fly, by design, and not the one that wants to tear itself apart with opposing forces."

He laughed again, joyously. Then he let go of her. And, contrarily, she now regretted the loss of his touch, when mere moments ago she'd been silently wishing he'd let her go.

She bit the inside of her lip as she confronted once more the clash of her feelings about the man.

"You radio home we were down and okay?"

She nodded. "They copied and reminded me we're… stuck. Until morning, at least."

"Yeah, I figured," Spence said as if it didn't bother him at all. "Everybody's out, even Dad and Uncle Will, on their own trip."

She hesitated then said, "I know they'd come get us if they knew, but I told Lakin not to interrupt them." For a moment, Spence just looked at her, and she started to feel uncomfortable. "I should have talked to you first, but Lakin told me what day it was and—"

"No. No, you did exactly the right thing." That Spence smile flashed again. "But then, you always do," he added, gesturing back toward the plane, "or we wouldn't be here talking about it."

Not for the first time, she thought she could hear the

difference in his voice between when they were talking like this and when he was chatting up some client who'd turned on the charm at her first sight of him. She'd like to think what she was hearing now was the real Spence, was sincerity, and all the rest was…well, not fake exactly—he wasn't a liar—but part of an act.

Hetty suddenly recalled the last time—and maybe *the* last time, given the gushing—she'd read a review of RTA on one of the travel websites: "Ladies, if you want some lovely scenery—and I don't mean just the landscape—check out RTA out of Shelby, and ask for Spence as your guide!"

She remembered how he'd deleted that last guest's phone number as soon as she was out the door, and how she had wondered if that's what he did with all of them.

What she should have been wondering about was why it mattered to her.

She knew he almost never left Alaska, only a couple of times to see friends down in Seattle. But even that was a while ago, and he'd said after the last time he doubted he would be going back because things weren't like they used to be.

She'd dwelt on that one for a while, too, wondering if it was a sign that Spence couldn't move on, if maybe he really was still that high school flirt. She'd later felt badly about those thoughts when she'd heard his dad talking about how the Seattle friends were all leaving the city for various reasons. She told herself sternly she needed to quit judging present-day Spence by the teenager she'd known. He'd proved her wrong then, when, on the edge of giving up, they had figured out how to use the quirk he did have to compensate for the one he didn't, but she hadn't learned, apparently.

You need to stop judging, period. Nobody appointed you judge or jury.

She came out of her reverie, almost embarrassed at having mentally wandered off. But at least this time it had served a purpose; the last of the adrenaline had ebbed and she was back to calm and steady.

As long as she stopped trying to figure out Spence Colton.

Chapter 8

Spence put the last crate in the bearproof—well, as much as anything was up here—storage outbuilding. He straightened up and spared a moment to be thankful that that was the last of it. It was quite a stretch from the beach to this hilltop campsite and, of course, the heavy-load part was on the uphill side. He needed to talk to Parker about some kind of motorized transport for the site, since it was one of their most established and often used destinations.

Too much for you, old man?

He could just hear Parker's laugh as he ragged on him for being a whole year older. He doubted his cousin dared do the same with his older brothers. Eli was too intimidating and Mitchell the same but in a different way. You took care with Mitchell because it was him you'd need if you were ever in trouble.

A faint sound from outside made him pause. Something in the distance, down toward the lake. It didn't repeat and he heard nothing else out of the ordinary. They hadn't seen any fishing boats on the water, but that didn't mean they weren't there now. Or hikers in the vicinity, though that would be beyond rare out here this early. Or simply a big elk getting fired up for a summer of fun.

Still, he stepped out of the building and looked down toward the water. He couldn't see the beach where the plane was tied off, but the part of the lake he could see was empty. He watched for a minute then went back to work. He stacked the crates in a logical—to him, anyway—order, settled them to be sure they were stacked solidly, then straightened, finally done. His back was probably going to remind him of this tomorrow.

Hey, at least you'll be around to be reminded. Thanks to Hetty, Ms. Cool Under Fire.

And now I get to look forward to—he glanced at his watch, the chronometer his dad had given him on his twenty-first birthday—*twelve more hours here, at least.* Twelve hours of unexpected leisure. Twelve hours he could spend fishing. Or hiking. Or paddling out on the lake. Since it never got really totally dark this time of year, the options were pretty open. Or he could take this gift of twelve hours and just relax.

Twelve hours with Hetty.

Sure. Relax.

He started walking around, inspecting the camp. Looking for something, anything, that needed attention. But everything seemed in working order. The tent—or the "tabin," as the little boy of one of their clients had called it once, a combination of tent and cabin—had no holes or rips, even the roof was clean. Which he of course knew, because he'd been the one to clean it when they'd taken it down last fall. The indoor woodstove was in good shape and vented properly. The camp stove outside was the same. Everything had wintered well.

So there, he'd killed a couple of those twelve hours. Now what?

Maybe he should radio headquarters. Ask Parker if there was anything he wanted done up here, as long as he was stuck anyway. He only had the basic tools that he always carried, back aboard the plane, and the tools that were always here, but he could make do, if his cousin had a project in mind. He'd be happy to tackle anything.

Anything that would keep him too occupied to think about being up here with Hetty for hours on end. All night. Alone.

All night. Damn.

He darted toward the tent. He'd lugged the folding camp beds down from storage along with the tent, without even thinking. But the original plan had been the big double one, for the honeymooning couple who would obviously be sleeping together. But there were a couple of singles, too, so he needed to be sure those were set up. And as far apart as possible. Hell, he should think about grabbing his sleeping bag out of the back of the plane and sleeping outside tonight. It wouldn't be that cold. And at least he might actually sleep, instead of lying awake all night, knowing she was just a few feet away.

Hetty was already inside. And she already had the singles unfolded and set up. On opposite sides of the tent. She glanced up as he came in, looked puzzled at his rush. He tried to think of something to say, something logical, reasonable. Words failed. There was something about standing in an area meant for sleeping, with Hetty Amos, that made him almost forget how to talk at all.

"Wood," he muttered finally. "We need firewood."

Her head turned as she looked at the woodstove and the neat rack of compressed-energy logs beside it. "There are ten of these, and they each last about two hours once it's going, don't they? And it's July, after all. Not like it's going to drop below zero."

"Kindling, then," he said almost desperately. And before she could question that, he turned on his heel and strode back outside. He knew perfectly well there was kindling and even some fire starters also there in the rack beside the woodstove, but he had to get away.

He tried to remember the last time they'd been alone together for any length of time. Usually there was family around, his or hers, or clients. And what time they did spend alone was usually filled with prep work, planning, or her doing her flight check while he got things loaded up. But now...

He stood outside on the hill, for one of the few times in his life too distracted to fully soak in the beauty all around him. Too distracted to savor the crisp, clean air, to gaze out at the expanse of the lake below, where the plane she had brilliantly brought down safely was just out of sight behind the edge of the stand of trees to the north.

He tried to tell himself he was so focused on her because she'd just saved them both with her skill. But he knew better. He was distracted because, when she was around, he seemed to lose control of his thoughts and they rocketed off in directions he should never be thinking. He was distracted because he knew it was futile, that she would probably forever see him as that kid she'd had to tutor in high school. He was distracted because she seemed only to dislike him now. Ironic, in a way, that she constantly ragged on him about flirting with clients when the only reason he did it was that the pull to do it with her was so strong.

And then the main source of that distraction came out of the tent cabin behind him.

"Adrenaline crash?" she asked as she halted beside him.

Startled, he looked at her. "What?"

"After an incident like this, I know the drained feeling that happens once the initial shock fades. You get kind of numb. And tired."

"Oh. Yeah," he said, gladly agreeing with her to avoid the real reason he was so…flustered.

Maybe that really was part of what was wrong with him. Maybe it was the letdown after a supremely stressful moment. Nothing like thinking you're going to die in a plane crash to get that adrenal gland going strong. Maybe it wasn't solely the idea of spending the night with her that had him so revved up and scattered at the same time.

Sure, Colton, keep telling yourself that.

"So…who's fixing dinner?" the ever-practical Hetty asked.

And now she'd disconcerted him again. "I… I sort of figured we'd just eat one of the prepacks," he said, referring to the bagged-and-sealed main courses with the long shelf life always kept in stock up here. "I saw there's some of that chili you like."

She was the one who looked surprised now. What, that he'd remembered she liked that particular version of the meals? Why would something that basic surprise her?

How would you feel if you knew I remember that you hate Brussels sprouts, that your favorite song is Hendrix's classic "All Along the Watchtower," and that your favorite

*color is that almost lime green of your jacket that makes
your eyes practically glow? Or that you want to see the
Eiffel Tower someday, after the Statue of Liberty, because
you like the French connection between them?*

His list of things he knew about her could go on and on.
Not because she'd ever told him all these things, but because
whenever he was around her he was glued to every word,
no matter who she was actually saying them to. Which was
almost always someone else, since she rarely spoke to him
directly other than on work-related things.

"—fine with me," she was saying, making him tune
back in. "I like it warm, though, so I'll get the fire going."

She turned to head back but paused for a moment, looking intently up the hill.

"What?" he asked.

Hetty shook her head. "Nothing. I saw something move
up there, or thought I did. But I don't see anything now."

"Maybe it was our moose, coming for a visit," he joked,
still trying to shake off the odd feelings he always seemed
to get when he was alone with her. "I'll go grab a couple of
those meals," he said, glad of the reason to take a hike, in
all senses of the saying. He also needed to grab the Kimber
out of the storage shed where he'd set it down to wrestle
with the bulky stuff. Nobody in their right mind would be
holed up this far into the Alaskan backcountry without a
weapon at hand to convince some of the local wildlife that
they would taste horrible.

They each turned to follow their stated intentions. But
before he'd taken two steps, Spence saw a chunk of bark fly
off the tree they were next to, for no apparent reason. A moment later, he heard a loud but distant crack of sound. Hetty

looked puzzled, but Spence knew. He knew, and he dived for her, taking her down to the ground in a fierce tackle. She tried to pull away, but he held her fast. He played it back in his head in an instant; the lesser sound of the impact with the tree and the loud report. He knew he was right.

"What—"

"That was a shot."

"There are always hunters around—"

"It was aimed at us."

Chapter 9

He was crazy. She'd heard the sound but assumed it had been a tree branch breaking, as often happened out here.

He was imagining things. That had to be it.

Except, Spence was far from crazy. He didn't go around imagining things. And when it came to almost anything here in the backcountry, at least on the ground, he had more experience than she'd ever have. And he'd certainly had more experience with firearms.

He was also lying on top of her. She was finding it a little hard to breathe and had a suspicion it wasn't solely because of his solid weight pressing down upon her. And he didn't seem to be breathing at all. Then she realized he'd lifted his head just slightly and tilted it as if listening. For another shot?

Another shot.

Someone had actually shot at them. She was beginning to get past the shock and process it now.

"Did they think we were a deer or something?" she asked, whispering by instinct as if the likely faraway shooter could hear her.

"Possible," Spence muttered. "But given where we were standing and that it came from further up the hill, not likely." His mouth curved into a wry half smile. "Not to mention the color of your jacket."

It was proof of how rattled she was that she hadn't even thought of that. Her lime-green puffy jacket would be hard to mistake for a deer or any other wild creature.

Some dirt a couple of feet away seemed to jump of its own accord and a moment later she heard the same kind of crack she'd heard before. And now that Spence had told her, it seemed obvious.

"He's not giving up," she said. "We need to move."

"My rifle's in the shed." He shifted as if he were about to get up.

"But that would be going toward him," she protested, a nightmare scenario flashing through her mind of Spence lying on the ground, bleeding out.

"The tent isn't going to stop a rifle round. Only other option is the plane, which is immobilized."

"But there's the radio," she said quickly, liking this idea much better. "Call for help."

"Which would take too long to get here to be much help."

"The plan is still more solid than the tent," she said. "It might not stop a bullet, but the walls of the plane would at least slow it down, wouldn't it?"

"Point taken," Spence said.

She felt a flash of relief at his agreement. She would feel better, safer, whether it was true or not, in her beloved plane.

A third shot hit the dirt, barely missing her left hip. She couldn't stop her instinctive flinch.

"We need to move," Spence said urgently. "Zigzag down to the big rock then cut right to the tree line."

Hetty nodded. "On three?"

She saw that familiar Spence grin that so captivated her flash for a split second. That he could do it under these circumstances impressed her more than she wanted to admit.

"On 'now,'" he said. "Like…*now!*"

She wasn't sure how he did it, but almost instantly he was on his feet and had pulled her up with him in one smooth, graceful move, reminding her yet again how strong he really was. How powerful.

And then they were running, and with the zigzag course he set, it was all she could do to both stay on her feet and keep up with him. It felt like a wild, wacky made-up game of some kind. Except for the very real threat as more shots rang out.

She felt a little safer as they passed the big rock and then dodged into the tree line. Something about the heavy cover of thick branches and solid trunks made this nightmare seem survivable.

"Is he just a bad shot?" she asked when they'd slowed slightly in the shelter of the big trees.

"Or maybe too far away," Spence said. "Given the time between the shots hitting and the sound, I'm hoping for the latter."

That made sense to her, since even she could hit a target if she was close enough.

"You piss anybody off lately?" he asked sourly.

"Only you," she countered, an edge in her voice; this was no time to be joking around. Even if you were Spence Colton.

He half turned to look at her. "You never piss me off. Irritate, yes, but full-on pissed? Nope."

She had the strangest feeling there was more depth to that seemingly teasing answer than he was letting show. Maybe it was the way he was looking her straight in the eye. But this was no time to get lost again in her meandering wonderings about Spence Colton.

They worked their way down to where the plane was beached. She stopped dead the moment it was in sight.

"It's further out," she said.

"Yeah," Spence agreed, and he didn't sound happy. "And I know I tied it off securely."

When they got close enough, she could see the mooring line must have come undone, allowing the plane to drift offshore a few yards, the line trailing through the water.

Her brow furrowed. She knew Spence was right. He'd never not make certain things were absolutely secure, so it had to have been untied, maybe even pushed free of the beach.

He didn't hesitate, even though he had to get wet again. Although, only knee-deep this time, just far enough to retrieve the rope and pull the plane back in. She ran to help, knowing a little extra weight on the line couldn't hurt. When the plane was beached again, and he was tying it off, she scrambled onto the float and then up into the cockpit, while Spence grabbed his emergency pack out of the bin in the back. Once she was in the pilot's seat, it took a moment for her to process what she was seeing.

Every reachable wire in the cockpit had either been yanked free or cut. Panels had been pulled free to expose more wiring, also cut. Most of the screens and dials had been smashed and every knob appeared broken off. She had little doubt, but tried the radio anyway. And got what she'd expected and feared. Nothing.

"What the hell?" Spence's words as he leaned into the cockpit were short, sharp and vehement. He almost immediately pulled back and looked around, scanning the water and landscape around them.

Hetty snapped out of her stunned state and realized he was looking for any trace of who had done this. The idea that the vandal might still be lurking around—and that there may be someone *additional* targeting them other than the shooter—terrified her. She wasn't normally so slow, but the impossible question of who would do this had rendered her normally sharp mind sluggish.

Was it the same person? Was the hand that had done this damage now holding the weapon that was firing at them? But why?

"Damn," Spence muttered. "That's what I heard."

"What?"

He didn't look at her when he answered, but kept scanning the area around them. "Back when I was stacking the crates in the shed, I heard…something. From down here. But I couldn't tell what it was, and it didn't repeat, so I figured it was probably a fishing boat in the area, or an elk or some other animal." His jaw tightened. "That'll teach me to assume."

"Do you think it's the same person who's shooting?"

"Out here this far, let's say the chance of it being two different people, one shooting at us, another destroying our means of communication, is pretty low."

"Unless they're working together."

His head snapped around to look at her. He grimaced and let out a compressed breath. "There is that," he muttered.

"But…why?"

"That's the big question, isn't it? There's nobody that—"

The lower right corner of the windshield shattered into a starburst. Spence dived sideways and down. He took her with him and they slid toward the floor. She gasped audibly. Had he been hit? For an instant, she froze at the idea. Then she erupted into motion. She squirmed around in the cramped space. Her heart slammed in her chest when she saw blood trickling down the side of his face.

"Stay down," he hissed.

She breathed again. He was alive. "How bad are you hurt?"

"I'm fine. We've got to move."

"But you're bleeding!"

As she said it, the blood reached his right eye and he swiped at it. He winced, but it seemed more in annoyance than pain.

"We've got to move," he repeated. "He knows we're here, and it sounds like he's using high-velocity rounds, so this isn't going to be a shelter after all."

He was clearly coherent and aware, so she shelved her immediate panic. "Move to where?"

He was silent for a moment, clearly thinking.

Hetty tried not to move, which was difficult. What was more difficult was ignoring the feel of Spence's body pressing down on her.

"Remember the cave?"

She knew immediately what he meant. Before they'd set up this semipermanent campsite, they'd explored the surrounding area thoroughly. "The one northwest of the camp?"

"Yes. If we can make it to the tree line, we can head west then up."

"All right."

"I'll take lead and you—"

"I will. You're hurt."

"I'm fine," he repeated.

"You're the one who's bleeding."

He swiped again at the trickle of blood on his face. "I just got nicked by some glass or something. It's just a—"

"If you say it's just a scratch, Spence Colton, I will knee you hard enough to make you scream."

She saw him realize she was in the perfect position beneath him to do just that. And to her surprise, he laughed. "That's my girl," he said.

Before she could ask what exactly he meant by that, he was moving.

Chapter 10

By the time they were halfway to the cave, Spence knew a couple of things. One, the shooter was either inexperienced with his weapon, or not at home out here. Was it because he was used to cities with lots of buildings, not trees with branches that moved with the wind? Used to more noise to cover his movements? Crowds to blend into? That, he didn't know. And it didn't matter. He only knew he was glad of it. Otherwise, one of those shots might have hit.

They scrambled up a steeper slope, still sheltered by the thick trees. He had only slung his pack over one shoulder initially, but now slid his other arm through the second strap. And aimed a rather fervent curse at himself again at the lack of his rifle usually secured on that side. If he had it, he could resolve whatever this was in a hurry.

The going was a bit rough, especially in spots where only a thin layer of earth covered larger—and more slippery—rocks. He'd gone down on a knee once already and it had been an effort to bite back the yelp of pain. But now that they were out in the open air, moving, any sound could easily carry to the hunter and betray their location.

He spared a split second to hope the guy had gone down a couple of times himself, but Spence never stopped moving. And Hetty, tough, stubborn woman that she was, kept up with him.

That last slip made him think of something else about the shooter. That maybe he was used to level ground—like asphalt or concrete—under his feet all the time. At this point, Spence would take any edge he could get, and that would definitely be one.

He paused to look around, to make sure he was headed in the right direction. It had been a while since he'd been up here. But if they made it to the cave, the situation would shift completely. With its entrance mostly masked by a large boulder and a huge Sitka spruce, most newcomers to the area would never realize it was there. The entrance was narrow, although the cave itself opened up quite a bit once you were inside. That meant anyone coming in after them would have to present themselves in the restricted space. Spence might not have his rifle, but he had his knife. He'd never used it on a human before, but if it came down to the assailant or him, he would.

If it came down to the assailant or Hetty, he'd not only use it but tear him up like a grizzly.

A faint rustling behind them made him spin around. Hetty froze in place. Spence visually searched down low, where the sound had come from.

"Stoat," he whispered to her, having spotted the small brown-and-white weasel in the underbrush. Summer was definitely here, since the wiry creature had shed its winter-white coat completely. It gave them a tilted-head assessing look and, apparently deciding they weren't worth any more attention, scampered off into the trees.

They moved on, carefully, stopping to listen every few

yards. They heard no more movement and, more importantly, no more shots. Had they lost the shooter? Spence didn't know for sure, and he wasn't about to gamble that they had. Not when the stakes could easily be Hetty's life.

Cursing himself once more for setting the rifle down in the storage shed—and hoping he lived through this, so he could never repeat that carelessness—Spence started moving again. The incline of the slope had lessened a bit, making the going easier, but the trees were also thicker, with branches barring almost every path, making moving silently and invisibly nearly impossible. Practically crawling—actually crawling would probably be a good idea—was the only answer.

He didn't stop to explain their pace to Hetty. She might not be a hunter, used to skulking around in the woods, but she knew they were under serious threat and she would understand why they were being so cautious. And why he was being so quiet. Besides, she knew this terrain almost as well as he did. That had been a requirement of working for RTA; to know the crucial things about where you were taking people who didn't know anything about it.

He thought of those days when he'd first been assigned—by his father, so he couldn't say no—to showing her to and around all their various destinations. One of the things he'd done was to teach her various hand signals. At that time, they had been intended to be used to avoid spooking game, or in the case of some of the critters of the wild, to avoid drawing their attention. Now he had to hope that she'd been paying attention to those lessons and remembered how to communicate silently.

The moment he had the thought, he almost laughed at himself. This was Hetty, and if there was one thing she consistently did, it was learn and remember. If that wasn't true, he wouldn't be here now. They'd both be in the drink, along with a crashed plane, probably both dead. But she'd pulled off a safe landing, saving them both.

And now here we are with some crazy person with a rifle trying to take us out, and I don't have a single damned idea who or why.

He stopped again, scanning ahead, searching for any sign of movement, listening for any sound. Then he felt a touch on his arm and quickly looked back at Hetty. She nodded to their left and slightly lower, making a motion with her hands at her head that it took him a moment to figure out. He couldn't stop his smile when he realized it was from back on that day when she'd asked if there were signals for particular animals and he'd jokingly put his hands up on both sides of his head to signify a moose's antlers.

He looked where she'd nodded, saw nothing at first. But Hetty also didn't make mistakes, so he waited. And after another minute or so, he saw movement: a large, brown, antlered head reaching down for some no-doubt tangy green summer growth.

They waited, watching. Most people who had never encountered one didn't realize the threat an angry moose could be. If he decided you were a problem he wanted to be rid of, you'd better get gone. And fast.

The big animal looked their way, as if he'd known they were there all along. And he probably had, Spence admitted. This was his neighborhood, not theirs, and any and all intruders were likely noticed, assessed and either ignored or driven out. And unlike their other pursuer, chances were good he wouldn't miss.

He went back to his meal and Spence looked at Hetty and nodded up the hill. Once more, they started inching their way forward. The moose looked again, but this time seemed satisfied that they were vacating the premises and stayed where he was.

Spence glanced back at Hetty and saw that she was smiling. She'd always loved it when they encountered the various wild creatures that inhabited—heck, owned—this countryside. She would never hunt them, but she loved to see and watch them. And apparently that hadn't changed.

Then again, Hetty didn't change much. Even in high school, she'd been like this—smart, quick and endlessly patient when necessary. She always had been that way with him, and he was sure he'd put quite a strain on those qualities, especially the patience, in those days. Heck, he was sure he put a strain on them now, although it was for completely different reasons.

At the time, it had been because he'd been sure, with all the certainty of a teenager, that nobody could help him. Hetty had proved him wrong, then. Now, it was because he had to keep some distance between them, otherwise he was going to say or do something utterly stupid and make it hard for them to work together. And they had to work together, because they were one of the main supports RTA was built on.

And so he kept his distance, upheld the front of flirting with every receptive female who came along, telling himself he had to maintain that space between them. He supposed it was the inner urge to do just the opposite that made him push the envelope, go further than he wanted to, which resulted in a weird feeling of both success and irritation when he succeeded in bringing on that disgusted eye roll of hers.

He shook off the tired old thoughts and speculation. He needed to be paying attention here. Just because there hadn't been any shots fired since they'd made it into the trees didn't mean the guy had given up. And wasting energy trying to figure out why wasn't helping, either. Right now that didn't matter, the why would come later. Assuming the shooter didn't find them and finish the job. He winced inwardly at the thought of his dad and uncle trying to figure out what had happened to them.

Once they were out of sight of the moose, he picked up the pace as much as he thought he could without advertising their presence. This plan obviously wasn't without risk, especially since they were essentially moving in the shooter's uphill direction, but if they made it to that cave, they'd at least have time to think and figure out what to do.

He paused at a break in the trees, to assess the two possible ways past the small clearing in front of them. He was trying to decide if they'd be better off heading to the left to get past that downed spruce or to the right on what looked to be a longer path that would keep them concealed among upright trees, when he heard…something.

His head snapped around and he held up a hand to stop Hetty. She froze where she was, about five feet behind him. He searched the direction of the sound—a faint snap, as if a branch had broken—had come from, but saw nothing; no movement, no moose, no human. He heard a faint sort of chattering—an animal—and wondered if it was the stoat and his clan. It sounded kind of weasel-like.

The area had fallen back into silence and still he waited.

Only when several minutes had gone by did he start to walk again. Hetty never protested, only moving when he finally lowered his hand.

At last, they reached the huge outcropping of rock he recognized. The cave was about midway along and he could see from their position that the huge Sitka spruce still stood. But the stretch from here to there was like the clearing down the hill. Too open for comfort.

He turned to Hetty and whispered, "I want to check and make sure the cave isn't…occupied."

It was unlikely, this late in the year and at this time of day, but still possible that some creature or creatures were sheltering there. The opening was too narrow for a bear of any size, but smaller wildlife had used the cave before, leaving evidence of nests, droppings and food debris behind.

"Okay," she answered just as quietly. "I'll go check on that little waterfall that was over there." She glanced to her right.

He remembered the small rivulet that ran down the south side of the rocks. He'd prefer she stay put, but he also knew they needed water. He was already thirsty after the long hike and she had to be, too. So, reluctantly, he nodded. Thought about saying, "Be careful," or some such other warning, but stopped himself. Hetty knew as well as he did to take care up here and not just because that shooter might still be in the area. She was aware that with one wrong step, she could take a tumble she wouldn't easily recover from. Especially as completely out of touch as they were now.

And then she was gone, moving as silently as he had been. Jaw set, he headed toward the cave. It was awkward, doing it in a crouch, but safer in case the shooter had perhaps spotted or heard them.

He made it to the cover of the big tree and took his first full breath. He edged around the slight outcropping of rock, hoping nothing had happened to block off their planned shelter's entrance. The narrow opening was just as he'd remembered. He stopped, listened, but heard nothing from inside. Still, he had his knife at the ready when he moved again. He had to find the perfect middle ground between stooping and staying constricted enough himself to get through it.

It was, thankfully, empty. There were signs that perhaps a coyote or three had wintered here, including bones leftover from whatever the clever carnivores had caught for several meals.

As long as we don't add any human bones to that pile...

His thoughts went immediately to Hetty and he turned to exit the cave. He needed to tell her they were good and to get her into the shelter. He didn't want her out there any longer than necessary. He could use a drink of that clear, mountain water himself, if the little creek was still running.

The moment he got back outside, he heard something. A sound that was half gasp, half scream. His entire body tensed.

An instant later, he heard a sharp unmistakable crack of sound.

Another shot.

And another scream.

Hetty.

Chapter 11

The fiery pain in her left thigh made her want to scream a third time, but Hetty knew that first loud gasp of shock and surprise was what had given her away. She hadn't been able to stop it, not after what she had found in the trees just past the tiny waterfall. She had the feeling the horrible image would be with her for the rest of her life.

Assuming she didn't bleed to death right here and now.

She couldn't get to her feet, was afraid she'd scream again if she even tried, so instead she rolled over, biting her lip fiercely to keep from crying out as her wounded leg took her weight for a moment.

Shot. She'd actually been shot.

She kept rolling, knowing the sooner she got out of sight in the trees, the better. The bullet had gone from the front of her thigh through the back, and she knew enough to know the exit wound would be the worst. But as far as she could tell, it hadn't hit the bone, so the big thing she had to worry about was the femoral artery. She kept as much pressure as she could on the wound while still getting herself under some kind of cover. She tried to blank the pain by concentrating on working out exactly what had happened.

She'd taken a grateful drink of the clear, cool water,

straightened and... Had she started back down yet? Or had she been in his line of fire simply by being at the waterfall? Had he known where it was and that, needing water, they would end up there? Had he spotted her and followed? Or had it just been chance that they'd both wound up within sight of each other?

Within sight.

That's what she should be thinking about. The fact that she'd seen him, although only a glimpse. Enough to tell he was indeed male, tall and with longish, wavy blond hair trailing down below the edge of what had looked like a knit cap. She thought she'd seen a mark on his face, a scar maybe, on his left cheek, but it could have just been a smear of something.

And he was wearing some sort of camouflage. The gray-and-black stuff. Which didn't work so well. She felt a spark of disdain for the man who clearly had thought it was always snow and rock here, when in fact so much burst into greenery this time of year.

She wondered if the guy—

"Hetty!"

It was a low but powerful sound, a whisper, yet projected all the way to where she was now lying in the shelter of the trees.

"Here," she answered, trying to get the same power into her voice as he had. She did, but only by letting some of the pain drive it. She thought she heard him swear, low and harsh, and knew he'd read the undertone.

It was probably less than a couple of minutes before he found her, although it seemed longer as she grasped at the bloody hole in her leg, still trying to stem the bleeding. He was on his knees beside her in an instant, edging her hands away from the wound.

"Spence, I found—"

"Shh. Let me check."

She hushed. Her apology for bringing this down on them could wait. So could the reason for it, for the moment. She concentrated on not screaming as he examined her leg. It took her a moment to realize what he was doing when at first he simply held her leg and watched it bleed, front and back.

"The artery?" she asked, trying not to let her fear into her voice.

"I don't think so. It's not pulsing, just bleeding. But it's bleeding a lot, and we've got to stop it."

He yanked off his belt free and wrapped it around her leg as a makeshift tourniquet.

"But he's out there—"

"I know." He tightened the belt hard enough she nearly moaned. "So we're moving right now."

"But I don't think I can—"

Before she could finish the sentence, Spence was picking her up. More easily than she would have thought possible given she was not a small woman at five-eight and she had a lot of muscle. She opened her mouth to protest but it died in her throat. If him carrying her hurt this much, it was obvious she couldn't walk. He got to his feet as if she weighed no more than that stoat they'd seen. Cradling her carefully, he started toward the cave.

It was a strange feeling for her, this helplessness. She'd fought it all her life, vowing at an early age to never be that helpless sort of female. Or, for that matter, male, like the scared-of-his-own-shadow kid from her first computer class back in high school. She'd felt an odd sort of pride that she hadn't been as nervous as he'd been, and never had been. Thanks to her mom and dad, she had more faith in herself than that boy'd had.

But now she didn't seem to have the strength to fight that helpless feeling. Or maybe it was just because it was Spence and she knew that, in this, she could trust him with her life. Because when the chips were down, Spence Colton would come through. He always had, and he always would.

Hetty surrendered to the weakness she'd always fought. She didn't ever want to be seen as weak, by anyone. She wanted to be like her mother, tough, strong, bending but never breaking no matter what life threw at her. But that was one more thing; Spence would never hold this against her, or throw it back at her the next time they fought over… well, the only thing they ever fought over.

She let her head rest against his shoulder, taking what comfort she could from his strength, his heat. The pain from her leg did not lessen, but it seemed to matter less at the moment. That was a marvelous knack he had. She'd seen him calm others when something happened on a trek. He always managed to take the edge off a situation, no matter what it was. He was especially good with kids, which she'd always found appealing.

Come on. You find everything about him appealing, except the fact that every other woman seems to feel the same way.

She'd never minded competition. In fact, she thrived on it in many arenas. Except this one. The one she couldn't handle: competing for attention from the man who had once been the tangled-up teenager she'd tutored in high school. The kid who had had to fight so hard to do what other kids their age did easily. The kid who had lit up when she'd made that crucial suggestion one day years ago and it had worked.

And three days later, after he'd practiced the visualization idea with words and sounds over the weekend, he'd showed up at their session and given her a huge, fierce hug that had made her breath stop and her heart race. She had—

She snapped out of the hazy reverie when she realized they were at the cave entrance.

"I'll set you down here. You hang on to my arm and try using your good leg to slip through. Stop there until I get in, and then we'll pick a spot for you to get off that leg."

It took her a moment to process what he was saying. It made perfect sense. It should have been easy to understand. Was she in shock? God, was she bleeding out? Was that why her head was fuzzy?

It took all she had to accomplish the simple thing he'd asked of her. And when she was inside, she had to lean on the cave wall to stay upright. Just seconds later, Spence was there and sweeping her up into his arms again.

To her surprise, he walked straight back then cut right slightly. He must have had time to explore a little or else he remembered the layout of the cave from the last time they'd been there. Knowing him, it was probably the latter.

A large piece of rock jutted out from the wall and he went past it. Then he stopped and lowered her gently.

"Why...?" she began, but didn't have the energy to finish asking why all the way back here, away from what light was coming through the entrance.

"If somebody just looks in from the entrance, they won't

see anything," he explained. With her current sluggishness, she didn't realize right away that she hadn't even gotten the question out, but he'd answered it anyway. As if he'd read her mind or something. And, for some reason, that gave her the strength to get out a complete thought this time.

"You think he could find it?" she asked, tamping down the apprehension that flared. "I mean we only found it that first time by accident."

"Depends on if they know the territory at all."

He didn't even look at her when he spoke, he was busy checking her wound. He loosened his belt around her leg. Even that made her clench her jaw. But there was something she needed to tell him.

"I don't think he does," she said. "I saw him, Spence."

He froze. Looked at her. She told him what little she knew, including about the color of his attire.

"Huh. You'd think somebody from here would know better," he said.

"Exactly what I was thinking."

"So maybe an import," he muttered as he shrugged his pack off. He dug into it, bringing out the red box that was his basic first-aid kit. He dug out what else he wanted, went back for one more thing, then, oddly, wrapped what looked like a wooden tongue depressor in gauze. He handed it to her.

"Bite down. This is going to hurt, and we don't want him to hear you."

"Think I'm going to scream?"

He gave her a solemn look. "I would."

She sighed. She'd had no room to talk, it had been her shocked cry, after all, that had drawn the shooter's attention. She had nobody to blame but herself for ending up lying here with that burning agony swirling out from her leg. But who wouldn't have done the same?

"I had reason, Spence," she said, rushing the words out. "There's a body out there, right by the waterfall."

He went still once more, this time in the act of using his knife—carefully sterilized with a wipe from the kit—to cut a bigger hole in her jeans so he could work on the wound. "He's already killed someone?"

"I don't think so. It looks like it's…been there a while. She. It's a woman. Half buried."

That information, that the body wasn't fresh, was apparently what he'd needed to shove the revelation into a compartment for later while he worked on the here and now. He'd always been good at that, too—putting things aside in order to tackle the present.

It turned out she did need the gauze-encased wood to clamp down on as he worked. The exit was the worst, and he used the one haemostatic sponge he had there to stop the worst of the bleeding. He used the kit's tourniquet up above the wound, a much better option than his belt. Then he dug out the roll of gauze and hoped there was enough.

When he was done, and the best bandage he could manage was in place, she let out an exhausted breath. The pain ebbed to a pulsing throb and she had to force herself to think.

"I don't think I can walk, not over the terrain here. And I know I couldn't keep up with you like this, even if I could walk."

"You're not even going to try," he said in a determined, decisive tone she'd only heard in tense situations. Situations where Spence did what was necessary. It was one of the things that had proved to her that the depth she'd first seen in him all those years ago was still there.

"I agree. So—"

"I slowed down the bleeding, but if you try walking, it'll be back to square one. You need medical attention."

It was as if he hadn't even heard her agree with him. Was he so used to her disagreeing with him he hadn't even noticed she wasn't? She spoke with more emphasis this time.

"I know that. So you'll have to go down past the lake until you can get a cell signal and let RTA know they need to get here ASAP."

He stopped with the debris from his work on her in his hand, which, at her words, had curled into a fist. "That's at least ten miles."

She gave him a puzzled look. A ten-mile hike in this wild country might be daunting to many, even most, but not to Spence. He did it for fun whenever he had a day off.

"I'm not leaving you alone here, unarmed, with a shooter out there. No way, Hetty, I'm just not."

Oh.

She felt heat rise to her cheeks, knew if they were out in the sun, it would show despite the darker tone of her skin. And if they were, she knew he'd notice. Mr. Sharp Eye never missed a thing. She turned her head instinctively, shielding her reaction to his words.

The movement shifted her balance, just slightly, but that was all it took to send a stabbing reminder through her leg. She winced, but managed not to cry out.

Spence's jaw tightened and he turned back to the first-aid kit.

He came up with a small paper packet of pills and a collapsed silicone circle. He tugged at the outer edge until it expanded into a small cup, then handed her the packet. "These should take the edge off. I'll go get some water for you to get them down."

Leave it to Spence to remember, even now, that she sometimes had trouble getting pills down. Then something else drove that out of her mind. "But he could still be there, watching that spot."

"I'll be careful." He hesitated then said, "And I need to go look at...what you found, anyway."

She should have known. Of course, he would. With a smothered sigh, she nodded. She looked at the pills then back at him.

"These won't make me groggy, will they?" That was the last thing she needed right now. She was having enough trouble keeping her act together, she didn't want to be drugged into more sluggishness.

"No, it's nonnarcotic. And like I said, it'll only take the edge off."

"That's all I need."

He gave her a smile that made her think of that moment in the plane when she'd threatened him with a knee applied to sensitive body parts and he'd laughed and said, "That's my girl."

And suddenly there was an ache inside her that almost surpassed the physical pain.

An ache that reminded her of just how long she'd been wishing that were true.

Chapter 12

It was hardly a waterfall, little more than you'd get from a healthy faucet, but it was consistent, clean and cold. She'd be able to get the pills down. Spence climbed the last few feet slowly, carefully. He scrounged a broken branch off the ground and tossed it ahead to see if it drew any fire from their invisible hunter. Nothing.

The Midnight Sun wouldn't allow for the cover of full darkness, but the tall trees made it seem darker than the perpetual summer twilight normally would, so while he could see, he was still on uneven ground and paid attention. Every couple of yards, he paused, listening carefully as he approached the small, clear spot around the rockslide that formed the path of the rivulet. Listening for any out-of-the-ordinary sound.

Like somebody reloading a rifle.

He suppressed a shudder as the image of the bullet wound in Hetty's leg slammed into his mind once more, shoving aside all else. He'd never seen her hurt or injured before, other than a sprained ankle she'd incurred playing basketball in school. After a beautiful, leaping dunk shot, she'd been jostled by an opposing player and come down wrong. Being Hetty, she'd made them tape up the ankle and gone back in to finish the game. Which they'd won, thanks to that shot of hers.

And during it all, she'd never let out a sound. She'd barely even winced. So that, if nothing else, told him the level of pain she was enduring now.

These won't make me groggy, will they?

Shot in the leg and she worried about that, when just about everybody else he knew would be asking for a large dose of groggy.

He scanned the ground around the small water flow and was starting to wonder if what she'd thought she'd seen had somehow been a trick of the light. If perhaps the trees had cast enough shadows in the everlasting twilight to make it seem as if—

And then he saw it himself. What she'd seen. *Who* she'd seen.

He swore under his breath.

The body was only partially buried, the head and arms— no, just one arm—were above ground. It was barely recognizable as a woman, and he was only guessing at that because what hair was left was long and wavy. Oddly, it also looked as if the tresses had once been spread out neatly, although now there were leaves and probably less benign things tangled in it. She'd been fed upon, which was hardly surprising out here.

He had to look away. He didn't think he was easily disturbed, but this did it. This desiccated corpse that looked as if it had been…arranged, got to him on more than one level. Then, as something belatedly registered, he glanced back, thinking he couldn't have seen what he thought he'd seen. But he had. The one arm that was above ground was the left. And encircling the bones of the left ring finger was a gaudy, huge diamond ring. Or at least something that was supposed to look like one.

The part of his brain that was still functioning was telling him the ring had to be fake. Because why else would whoever had put this woman here leave the diamond behind if it were real? If it was, the piece would be worth tens of thousands, and he just couldn't see a killer walking away from that. So whoever had left her here, with that ring, either hadn't known or hadn't cared.

Or…had put it there on purpose?

He gave a sharp shake of his head and yanked his gaze over to the calming trickle of the waterfall. It seemed pristine…untouched, but what wouldn't after that sight? No wonder Hetty had screamed. He almost had, and he'd known what to expect. Well, almost; he'd never seen a body like this, in this decomposed condition, but at least he'd known it was there. Thanks to poor Hetty.

He grabbed his cell phone. It might not get a signal here, but the camera still worked. Not for nothing did he have a sister and cousin in law enforcement, who often spoke of crime scene photos and how the sooner they were taken, the better. Obviously this poor woman had been here a while, but still… Besides, putting the phone between him and the ugly scene made looking at it a tiny bit easier.

After taking several images from several angles, he shoved the phone back in his pocket, went and took a long drink from the stream himself, then filled the cup and headed back to the cave. And wondered all the way if whoever was after them now had something to do with that corpse. Was he protecting this site, afraid if the body was found, so would he be? Had he chosen this place because of its remoteness?

Or were the two totally unconnected? Was it just a freak accident that had left a body half buried there? Was this anonymous gunman hunting them for some other nefarious reason? That didn't seem likely, as Spence could think of no reason for someone to shoot at him or Hetty, but he freely admitted he might not be thinking with total clarity.

He tried to go carefully, quietly, keeping hidden, but he was suddenly in a rush to get to Hetty. When he got back to the cave, he gave her the water and watched as she downed the pills. As soon as she had, she looked at him carefully.

"You found her."

"Yes."

"You agree it's...a woman?"

"I think so."

"How long do you suppose she's been there?"

He grimaced. "No idea. I think freezing temperatures affect...decomposition. And up until a couple of months ago, we were still getting three or four feet of snow up here."

Hetty lowered her eyes and he thought he saw her shudder. "It was...awful."

"Yes," he agreed softly. "Sometimes I don't know how my sister does what she does, or my cousin."

The thought he'd shoved aside while focused on the unsightly discovery came back to him now. The reality of what he'd been looking at, the dead body half buried on an Alaskan hillside, had made the memory of the Colton family tragedy fade, but now it came back. Hard.

His expression must have changed because she asked, "What?"

"I was just remembering…a family story." He hesitated, but decided it may be a good distraction. For her, from the pain and the shock, and for him, from the long night ahead alone with Hetty. "Did you know I had an aunt?"

Her brow wrinkled. "I remember your dad mentioning his sister who died, before they ever came here, before you were born. And Lakin told me that was the reason for the fishing trip with your dad and uncle."

"Aunt Caroline was the reason they left San Diego."

"That's quite a switch, from sunny San Diego to Alaska."

"They needed a big change." He paused, took a deep breath and went on. "Because in San Diego, my aunt and my grandparents were murdered."

Hetty let out a shocked gasp. "Spence," she said with a shake of her head. "I didn't know that."

"They don't talk about it much anymore."

"Who did it? Did they…ever catch him?"

"They did. His name was Jason Stevens. He was an ob-sessed fan of my aunt's."

"Fan? She was famous?"

"When she was still in high school, Caroline was…dis-covered, I guess they call it. She became a model and was very successful very fast. Did a lot of ads, until it seemed like her picture was everywhere. And with that came a lot of attention, not all of it good. Stevens stalked her for months, and she was a wreck over it, my dad says. But… their parents didn't take it seriously."

He had to stop for a moment. He'd never known his aunt, but he'd been very aware of the pain of his father and his uncle during the first few years of his own life, when they were trying to rebuild here in Alaska. Hetty, bless her, didn't push or prod, she simply waited, silently. Bracing himself, he went on.

"The police found his journal, and he'd been planning this for over a year. His delusion was that Caroline was his girlfriend and her parents were keeping her away from him. The original plan was to break in, kill them and take her away with him. He got the first part done. He stabbed them to death in their own bed. Then he drugged Caroline, dressed her and started to carry her out of the house. But…she woke up."

"And she fought," Hetty said softly. "She was a Colton, so she fought."

It was odd, to feel a spark of warmth amid this shocking, sorry tale, but her words had done it. He was also a little puzzled that she hadn't yet asked why he was telling her all this. But now that he'd started, he kept on. Because if there was anyone he knew who would listen and understand, it was Hetty.

"Yes, she did. And he ended up strangling her to death. Then he put her on the living room couch, sat down beside her and arranged them in…a loving pose. Then he committed suicide with an overdose of what he'd drugged her with. Uncle Will and Eli found them."

Her eyes widened even further, reflecting what light there was. "No wonder Eli does what he does."

Spence nodded. "Took me a while to put the two together, but yeah."

"You weren't even born when all this happened."

"No. And they didn't talk about it, like I said."

"Too painful," she guessed. "I'm so sorry, Spence."

He shrugged. It wasn't burrowed as deep into his psyche

as it was with his father, Uncle Will and Eli, who had been eight years old at the time. Mitchell had been barely five and Parker only a baby, so their experience was much like Spence's. But Eli had been older, and had been at the scene. He used to think he could never imagine what it must have been like for his cousin to see those bodies.

Now he had a much clearer idea. He was going to carry the image of that woman out there for the rest of his life.

"Anyway," Spence went on, trying to shake it all off, "that's it. The press never quit on it, harassing the family, even showing up at Eli's school, so they finally packed it in and moved here."

"I'm glad about that part."

Hetty hadn't sounded like herself when she'd said it. In fact, she'd sounded almost shy. He wanted to interpret her words as she was glad he was there. But big as his ego was, he couldn't quite do it. And she went on so quickly, changing the subject, he was sure he was right.

"I wonder…do you think that woman out there might be someone authorities were looking for and never found?"

"Could be. That's what I was thinking, so I took some pictures." Her eyes widened and he hastened to explain. "Something I picked up from Kansas. They need a record of the scene."

She nodded in understanding and gave him a small smile. "Kansas taught you well."

"She's just always talked about not disturbing the scene if they find…someone dead."

That Hetty could have also died, had the assailant been a better shot, was something he didn't want to dwell on. He went over to where he'd dropped his backpack and dug for a couple of the emergency ration bars he always carried. There was a pack of twelve inside, which was enough to get them both through until somebody from RTA got to the site.

At least you didn't leave the pack in the shed, idiot. Spence sighed in frustration.

"What's wrong?" Hetty asked.

His anger at himself must have showed on his face.

"Nothing," he said sourly. "Other than the fact that I could have taken that guy out by now if I hadn't left the damned rifle in the shed." He doubted he'd ever forgive himself for that.

"There was no reason to expect…this."

He grimaced. "And what's that saying that's practically the state motto? Expect the unexpected?"

"'North to the Future' isn't doing it for you, huh?"

The grimace became a tight, wry half smile. "Not at the moment, no."

"We'll be fine," she said quietly. "RTA will be here in the morning, and we'll be back home by noon, I bet."

"Maybe."

"We'll probably hear them when they arrive. You know how sound carries up the hill out here."

"Yeah."

"Spence, stop blaming yourself. Frankly, I'm much happier waiting it out here than having you out there hunting something that can shoot back."

There was no doubting the genuine concern in her voice. He knew what he wanted to think, but quickly quashed it, telling himself it wasn't that she'd be worried about him, she just didn't like the idea of being left here alone, injured and pretty much immobilized. And who would?

He dug back into the pack and pulled out the emergency blanket. If it was just him, he wouldn't worry about it this time of year, in the shelter of the cave. But Hetty was hurt, and she'd lost enough blood she could get colder than normal, and faster. He also dug out the small pack of candles. It might not get dark outside this time of year, but it was pretty dim in this protected corner of the cave.

"That's my boy," she said. He turned back sharply. "Always prepared."

As she echoed his earlier sentiment, his rattled brain rocketed to other circumstances where that might be an appropriate statement. Circumstances he'd never be in with Hetty, no matter how much he might want to be.

He managed a rather tight smile. Then he studied her for a moment. She looked a little better, the furrow on her forehead had smoothed out a bit. "Feeling better?"

She nodded. "Those pills did take the edge off." She looked at the things he'd brought over to where she was propped against one wall of the cave niche. "You're going to have to restock when we get back."

"Yeah." He always made sure the backpack was ready to go, and he personally tested everything in it himself, so he'd know exactly what he had to draw upon.

"When was the last time you did one of your survival jaunts?"

He didn't like her using the word survival at the moment, but answered simply. "Spring. But early, when it was still cold enough to really test things."

"You mean when it only gets down into the twenties instead of the teens?"

"Or negative numbers. I'm careful, not crazy."

She laughed then winced as if it had hurt, and all his amusement vanished. He was down on his knees beside her in an instant. "Hetty?"

"I'm all right," she said, although she sounded a tiny bit breathless. "I just…jostled it, I think." She glanced at the blanket. "I do think we may need that later, though."

We? He'd planned on putting it just over her tonight, but now that she'd said that—and once he got the delicious idea of snuggling with her under one blanket out of his head— he knew she had a point. The reflective blanket did reflect body heat, after all. That was the whole point of it, and so he should add his own heat, for her sake.

So he would find himself in the position he'd always longed for but never expected to have. Snuggled up to Hetty Amos, under a single blanket, in what dark there was, with practically zero chance of interruption. And imagining what might be happening if she wasn't hurt.

It was going to be a hell of a night.

Chapter 13

"Talk to me," Hetty said, not liking this strange feeling that was overtaking her. Every little sound made her pulse kick up, which in turn made her oddly lightheaded, which then scared her even more.

She wasn't used to being scared. And telling herself she wasn't used to being shot, either, wasn't helping much.

"About what?" Spence asked, sounding wary.

"Anything. Everything. I just don't want to fixate on what happened when I can't seem to think straight."

"You were shot, Hetty. Of course you can't."

She was pretty sure Spence would be handling it better. She'd bet his brain wouldn't have disintegrated into turmoil, bouncing from here to there to over there, unable to settle on any one thought or idea.

"Talk about something else. Tell me about… I don't know, tell me about Gwen."

He blinked. At least, she thought he did; it was pretty dark back here, and he'd said he didn't want to light one of the candles unless they had to. But she hated that she couldn't see well enough to really read him, as she usually could.

Or thought she could.

"Uh…who?"

Despite everything, she almost laughed. "Gwendolyn Merchant? The woman so entranced with you she demanded you take her phone number?"

"Oh. Her."

Hetty couldn't deny the fact that his apparent inability to remember the woman's name had made her feel oddly better.

"She'd be crushed," she said, trying to make her tone light and teasing. "She thought you were entranced with her."

She was able to see him shrug then. "It's an act. It's always an act."

He'd never actually admitted that before and she felt further mollified by his admission. And before she thought—she seemed to be having trouble with that at the moment—she asked, "Why?"

"Protection."

She heard him suck in a sharp breath, and thought she heard a muttered oath, low and harsh. As if he hadn't meant to let that out and regretted that he had.

"From what?" she asked.

"Never mind."

"Sorry, you don't get to call that back."

The idea that Spence Colton thought he needed protection from anything was rather unsettling, and went entirely against the mask he usually presented. The flirting, the lightheartedness, the certainty verging on the edge of cockiness but with none of the obnoxious aspects. Which left her with one big question.

What could the brilliant, handsome Spence Colton need protection from?

His response to the question turned out to be total silence. He went back to the cave entrance periodically, she supposed to look and listen. Each time he returned and she asked, he shook his head to indicate there had been nothing to see or hear. But he still didn't speak.

She was starting to feel a little fuzzy-headed. She supposed a combination of it being well after midnight now and the chill starting to take effect. Plus that little fact that she'd been shot.

"You cold?"

Later, Hetty thought, she'd appreciate that it was concern for her that had made him break his self-imposed silence. But right now she was too busy realizing he was right.

"Yes," she said, barely suppressing a shiver.

He reached for the emergency blanket. The next thing she knew, he was lying next to her, arranging the blanket over them both. Loaning her his body heat. Her slightly dizzy mind wanted to romp off in ridiculous directions at that idea, so she bit her lip to remind herself to keep her thoughts to herself and her mouth shut.

She savored his warmth, only then realizing how cold she'd actually become.

"Thanks," she murmured.

"Mmm."

Nice, noncommittal response. They lapsed back into silence.

She didn't know how much time had passed when Spence finally spoke. Quietly, softly, soft enough that she could probably have slept through it, had she been asleep.

But the sleep she'd assumed would be easy to come by seemed to have vanished the moment he had laid down and wrapped the blanket—and himself—around her.

"Do you remember," he whispered, "what I was like when you first started to tutor me?"

As if she could forget, even if it had been over a decade ago. "You haven't changed all that much," she said.

"I know. Always a smart-ass."

"I didn't mean that. I mean you still work hard, and when you find something that works for you, you run with it. You're brilliant. You just had to find a way to express that in terms the rest of the world could understand, and find a way to understand how they express things."

He'd gone very still. She didn't even think he was breathing for a moment. Finally, he said, in an almost awed tone, "You thought that? Back then?"

"I knew it," she said with a shrug she knew he'd feel even though he couldn't see it.

"You never made me feel stupid, like others did."

"Because I knew you weren't. I knew you weren't just a pretty face."

"I…played on that. The looks and the flirting, I mean. It was part of it." Another pause before he said, "That's what I meant about protection. It was the…façade, I guess. Shelter. The looks were just part of the act, part of the cocky wise-ass routine that kept people from seeing the real me. The stupid me I always thought I was until you showed me another way."

Hetty felt a fierce, aching tightness in her chest. She'd known he was grateful to her for pointing him in the direction that had enabled him to break free, but she hadn't known how much of his attitude was based in this. Beyond curious, she had to ask.

"And the flirting now?"

"Habit, I guess. And still a bit of that protection. Because it's obvious I'm not serious."

"You might want to rethink that," Hetty said dryly. "Because I'm pretty sure some of our clients thought you were serious."

"You saying I'm too good at it?" There was a touch of teasing in his tone.

"Too good for my comfort," she admitted.

He went utterly still again. "Why?"

She couldn't tell him the truth. She just couldn't. So she dodged. "It's uncomfortable to be around."

"It's not easy to do," he said. "Especially when one of the things it's covering up is…my real feelings. About somebody else. But I don't know how to act around a woman when the feelings are…real. I never have. So she has no idea."

It was her turn to go still. There was somebody else? Someone he had real, genuine feelings for? She couldn't stop herself from asking, "Who?"

"Somebody I've had a crush on for a long time." She heard his deep intake of breath. Felt his body tense, as if he were steeling himself for a blow. "Like since the eleventh grade."

Eleventh grade. When she had begun to tutor him. Surely, he wasn't saying…what she wished he was saying. It had to have been someone else.

"Where is she now?" she asked, trying for a merely curious tone.

Again there was a pause and a renewed tensing. And then he said it. "Right here."

Her breath slammed to a halt in her throat. She couldn't speak.

He went on. "In my arms. At last." And then the old, smart-aleck Spence reappeared. "Of course, she didn't have much choice."

She swallowed. Gathered her nerve. Spared a second to think how it figured that they would reach this point here, in this remote place in this backcountry they both loved, trapped in a freaking cave, waiting for rescue. And then, knowing she had to at least match his courage, she said it.

"If she'd had a choice, she would have chosen this."

It was another silent moment, one in which she could still feel his tension. He raised up on one elbow before he said, tentatively, "Hetty? You…mean that?"

"I think…it's why I get snarky with you so often."

He reached out with his free hand, brushed the back of his fingers over her cheek. "I never knew. Never dared to even hope. And I was afraid I'd…ruin our friendship, so I really locked it down."

She looked up at him, able only to see a profile in the dim light. She thought she would have recognized him anyway, even if she hadn't known it was him next to her. Hadn't she memorized his face all those years ago? And he truly hadn't changed that much on the outside, either. His jaw stronger, more masculine, the line of him lean, having lost any lingering softness of youth.

"And I'm just me, and you were a Colton, the big name in town."

He let out a wry chuckle. "I love my family, and I'm

proud of what they've built, who they've all become, but sometimes it's a pain in the backside."

She couldn't help smiling, widely. "It's only me. You can say ass."

The chuckle became a laugh this time. Then he dropped back down off his elbow and wrapped his arms around her again. "And that's another reason," he said, sounding both amused and delighted.

And genuine. More important to her than anything, there was no doubting the utter sincerity in his voice.

Spence Colton may have been a flirt in front of her countless times, but never had he ever given any of those women the authenticity and certainty he'd just given her.

Where they went from here, she didn't know. And right now she was too weary to think about it. It was simply enough to lie there, wrapped in his arms and the blanket that so nicely reflected their body heat back to them.

And imagine a night when they might generate an entirely different kind of body heat.

Chapter 14

Spence was in the middle of a strange daze…half awake, half asleep. The asleep part of his brain was manufacturing a crazy dream in which the thunder of a running herd of moose somehow morphed into the steady thwap-thwap sound of a rotor blade.

A big rotor blade.

A helicopter.

The moment the sound registered in the half-awake part of his brain, he jolted upright. Hetty didn't wake, so he tried to move carefully, until he was clear and could make his way to the cave entrance.

He had to step out into the small clearing to get away from the echo from inside the cave walls. He scanned what sky he could see, much brighter now that it was nearly five in the morning and the sun that never set was higher in the sky.

Bless RTA, someone had to have rolled out the moment it was safe to fly by sight.

Spence could still hear the helicopter, but it sounded like it was down by the water. That made sense, if it was the RTA chopper, which was the only thing that made sense. And then he caught a glimpse as the bird rose and became visible above the trees downhill from him. He recognized the Bell Jet Ranger instantly, the RTA logo clear on the side, matching the one on the plane.

He ran back into the cave, smiling as he dug into his backpack.

"They're here," he said quickly when he realized Hetty was stirring, raising up on one elbow and looking toward him. "Don't know who's flying, but it's the RTA bird."

He grabbed the two things he needed and raced back outside. He turned on the small walkie-talkie. Used mainly for contact when they were working with a large group and more than one guide, for the guides to keep in touch if they were out of sightline, it didn't have the greatest range, but it might just reach the radio on the helicopter.

He held the walkie up to his mouth, keyed it and spoke, using his initials as his moniker, as usual.

"RTA bird, this is SC. Do you copy?"

Nothing but dead air. He waited until the helicopter made another circle, obviously scoping things out before making a landing. When it was at its closest point to him, he tried again. This time, the walkie-talkie crackled back.

"SC, this is RTA One." Spence had never been so relieved to hear his father's voice. "Your location?" Ryan Colton asked.

"Northwest of you. I'll fire a flare, but I don't think there's room for you to land up here."

"Fire."

He aimed the small flare gun he'd retrieved from the backpack upward, straight, for a more accurate pointer. He fired it, the little rocket soaring and trailing a stream of red smoke.

"Got it," his father said. A moment later, the helicopter was directly overhead, hovering. Spence waved widely. And this time the audio on the walkie-talkie was much clearer. "You're correct on the landing. You'll have to meet me back by the plane."

"Hetty's hurt, Dad." He started to explain then realized his father didn't know yet about the shooter. "And be on the lookout," he said sharply. "There was somebody out here either playing some kind of twisted game taking potshots, or trying to kill us."

"What?" His father's voice was harsh.

"No sign of him since last night, but be aware. You're armed?"

"Of course. Can you get her to where you beached?"

"I'll manage. We'll start now, but it'll be slow."

"And be careful," Dad said warningly.

"Absolutely."

On his way back he detoured momentarily to the site of the body, thought a moment longer about the idea that had struck him, then reached into his pocket for the little packet he'd grabbed. He crouched down beside the hand with the ring. If this was a mistake, he'd have to live with it, he thought.

When he was done he straightened, and headed quickly back uphill. When he got into the cave he found Hetty had struggled to her feet, although she was extremely wobbly. She tried to stand straight as he ran over to her, taking her arm to steady her.

"Take it easy," he said. "It's Dad, and he knows the situation. He can't land here, so we have to head back to the beach, by the plane."

She only nodded. She was trying to fold up the blanket, but he grabbed it and what was left of the four emergency ration bars he'd taken out, and stuffed it all into the pack. He'd straighten things out and restock the bag when they got to base. Or maybe the next day, after he'd had about twelve hours of sleep and time to recuperate from the terrifying fear of losing Hetty.

Once he had the backpack settled on his shoulders, he turned to look at Hetty. She was propping herself up against a cave wall, but, even so, looked far too unsteady for his comfort.

"Don't get mad at me…" he began.

"I've sworn off." She managed a smile, but it was a bit wobbly. "Temporarily anyway."

"Good. Because we need to get back to the beach ASAP, and you trying to walk is going to really slow us up." He didn't mention it could well start her bleeding again, and she'd already lost too much.

"I can—"

He cut her off. "I have no doubt you could, if you had to. But you don't have to, Hetty. You're not alone."

That was when he moved and, in one swift but very careful motion, picked her up in his arms, settling her against him as he had before.

"Spence, no," she protested. "From where I was shot to here is one thing, but all the way back—"

"Hush." He pushed away the errant thought that he would like to hush her by kissing her so hard and deep she couldn't talk. But this was hardly the time, and she was in no condition. And he was starting to wish he'd never let loose his feelings to her last night, because they seemed to think they now had free rein. "It'll be fine."

He knew it would be. She was no lightweight. She was only about four inches shorter than his own six feet, and she was fit, with lots of muscle, but now that getting her out of here and to medical help was within reach, he felt like he could run a marathon carrying her. He just had to hope the adrenaline pouring through him would last long enough to get her to the helicopter.

It was tough going, and having to make sure there was enough clearance between the trees to get her long-legged frame through without jostling her wound, made it even trickier. Plus he had to be alert to everything around them, just in case the shooter really was still around.

He didn't know how long it really took, but it seemed far too long before they broke clear of the tree line and he saw the RTA helicopter sitting in the clearing above the beach where the plane was tied off, just as they'd left it. And climbing out of the plane's cockpit was his father. As nimble as ever, Ryan Colton jumped from the portside float to the beach and headed toward them at a run.

When he reached them, Spence could see his father's expression was grim and angry. He'd obviously seen the mess in the cockpit, the bullet hole, the ripped-up control panel, broken dials and destroyed radio. But he took one look at Hetty and instantly his loving father was back.

"Don't you worry, Hetty. I radioed ahead to the trauma center and they're on standby for us. You'll be fine."

She managed to smile at the man who was acting more like doting parent than boss at present. "I'm okay. I just feel a little woozy, that's all."

Spence wanted to hold her the entire way, but it wasn't practical inside the 'copter. So they stretched her out on the second row of seats, secured her as best they could, and his father went back to the controls.

Dad glanced at him, gaze fastening on the cut on his forehead.

"I'm fine," he said before he could ask. "It's just a cut from the glass, I think."

"You'll need to strap in for takeoff," his father said with a nod toward the copilot's seat as he put the headset back on. Then he gave Spence a sideways look. "After we're airborne, you can get up to check on her every five minutes if you need to, but you buckle up the rest of the time."

"Yes, sir," Spence said, because when Ryan Colton gave an order in that tone, that's what you did. And he had to admit, he felt a little comforted when he watched his father's competent hands work so swiftly. He put on the copilot headset, but kept one ear clear so he could hear any sound from the back.

"Hey, it could have been worse," Dad joked, clearly trying to lighten things up. "You could have really crashed."

"With Hetty flying?" Spence said. "Not a chance."

"Good point. Okay then, you could be driving."

Spence gave a half-hearted laugh at his dad's obvious try at Alaskan humor—applicable because driving to a medical facility would be impossible due to the simple fact of no roads that didn't take them a hundred or more miles out of their way.

And hours of time Hetty might not have.

He'd noticed that there had been some fresh blood at the wound site when they'd put her down across the three seats that formed a bench in the back. Not a lot, but any was too much as far as he was concerned.

"Dad?" he said quietly. His father looked at him as the rotor picked up speed and volume. Spence couldn't help the tightly wound tension in his voice when he added one word. "Hurry."

"All possible speed," Dad promised, and Spence knew he meant it. And it wasn't just because Hetty was a crucial part of RTA. She was, but she was also a part of the extended Colton family. And if there was one thing he was utterly positive about in life, it was that Coltons came through for family.

It was a lesson they'd learned the hard way.

Chapter 15

As promised, staff at the trauma center was ready and waiting. There was no helipad per se, just a marked-off area in the parking lot. With his typical skill, Dad set the bird down so gently, Spence wasn't even positive they were down until the crew with the gurney started heading toward them.

They handled her as gently as he ordered them to. He caught Hetty watching him as he gave that order. She had an odd look on her face, and somehow he knew she was thinking of those hours last night when feelings they'd kept buried for over a decade had broken free. Once she was up and around, they would have to go there again, but for once he didn't dread what would surely be a talk with a capital T.

Hetty didn't hate him.

The moment when they wheeled her past those swinging doors and they closed after her, shutting him off from what would happen next, put him in mind of a million movie and TV scenes. In reality, he felt more than a bit nauseous, his gut churning as she disappeared. One of the staff asked if the cut on his forehead needed attention, but he said no. Nothing mattered right now but Hetty.

He stood there staring at those closed doors for what

seemed like a long time. Then he started pacing. Dad appeared with a cup of hot coffee. He drank it for the jolt, if nothing else.

It seemed like forever before someone came out to talk to them. A weary-looking woman with the hospital cap holding back graying dark hair. "It missed the artery and there doesn't appear to be any damage to the femur. She got lucky there," she said, "but she's still lost a lot of blood. We're transfusing now."

"If you need more…" Spence began, but the doctor, whose name tag said "W. Masters" followed by some letters he had no idea the meaning of, shook her head.

"Not for her, but donations are always welcome at the blood center." It sounded like something she was saying by rote, but he supposed that was a reflexive, and normal, request for an ER doctor. "We found no pieces of the bullet, and cleaned out all the other debris that we found, which should hopefully prevent infection. We've placed a drain for now. We'll be moving her into the ICU. You won't be able to see her for a while, so see to yourself for the moment, Mr. Colton."

When she'd gone, his father put an arm around his shoulders.

"Come on, let's go outside. I think you need a bit of non-hospital-smelling air."

He couldn't deny that, but couldn't seem to remember how to move. Dad had to practically push him toward the doors. Once they were outside, he automatically sucked in a long, deep breath. He closed his eyes for a moment, as if that could make it all go away, but it only brought the image of Hetty, down and bleeding, vividly back into his mind.

"She's a tough girl, Spence. She'll be all right." Spence looked at his dad in time to see him grimace. "And in the meantime, I'm sure there will be some folks with badges who will need to talk with you eventually."

The rest of what had happened out there slammed back into him. "Dad... Hetty found a body out there."

Ryan Colton went rigidly still. "This guy killed somebody else?"

"Not unless he's been at it and gotten away with it for a while. That body was...not fresh."

Spence could almost see his dad processing, and thought he should get it all out before he had to spend what would probably be a couple of hours with the state troopers. So he quickly poured out the whole story. He watched his father frown at the news of the plane's engine losing power then smile briefly at Hetty, getting them down safely. Ryan frowned again hearing about the shots fired near the campsite, the plane's radio being taken out, the shots fired there, their escape, and finally what Hetty had seen in the moments before she'd been shot.

"She saw the guy?"

"At a distance, but yeah."

"Does he know she saw him?"

"I...don't know. I was..."

"Preoccupied with keeping her alive overnight. I get it, son." He looked past Spence suddenly, and when he turned to see what had caught his eye, Spence saw two men headed their way, one in uniform, one not.

Dad nodded slowly. "I see they've already notified the authorities."

"Gunshot wound, I think they have to."

"Probably," his father agreed, watching the two men approach.

"I was half expecting Eli," Spence said with a grimace.

"If they knew about the body, it probably would be him," Dad said.

Spence guessed he was right. Crimes didn't get much more major than murder, and as a lieutenant in the Major Crimes Unit of the Alaska Bureau of Investigation, his cousin Eli Colton, a big believer in being involved, had a lot of say in when and where he got assigned to cases. In fact, he wouldn't be surprised if the Colton name was what had netted them a two-person response instead of just the local in uniform.

"So once they find out…" he began then stopped as the men got nearer.

"We'll likely be seeing him," dad agreed.

The two men reached them and stopped. Both Spence and his father nodded to the one in the Shelby PD uniform. Bobby Reynolds was familiar to them both; they'd dealt with him on a few occasions back in Shelby. For him to be here now, he must have come in by air, maybe on a state agency bird. The man shoved a hand through his light brown hair and there was what appeared to be genuine concern in his face and voice when he spoke.

"How's your flygirl?"

"She's going to be fine," Spence said firmly.

Reynolds nodded then introduced the man in plain clothes as Detective Sam Barton, from the Alaska State Troopers. Since Alaska had no counties, there was no county sheriff to turn to, and the AST handled…well, almost everything.

"Mr. Colton, Mr. Colton…you're Eli's uncle and cousin?" Barton asked.

"Yes," Dad said.

"He's a good man," the investigator said.

"He is," Ryan confirmed.

Then Barton shifted his attention to Spence, but without, Spence noted, asking Dad to leave them alone. The Colton name again, he guessed.

"Obviously, we'll need some details about what happened up there," Barton said. He nodded toward the small park across the street, fairly empty at this early hour, although Spence knew it would fill up later as people rolled out to enjoy the predicted summer weather for the week. Of course, any of the locals could tell you weather predictions for the area were notoriously inaccurate and to be taken with a pound of salt. He remembered the day when it had been sunny in town, windy out on the sound and snowing up in the pass. None of which had been predicted.

They found an empty picnic table in the park and sat down.

"This guy had a rifle?" Barton asked.

"Yeah. High-power, I'd guess." He grimaced. "Didn't have time to dig out a spent round for you, but there's one in the cabin of the plane, somewhere in the back. And I can get you to a tree I think has another one buried deep."

Barton looked appreciative. "Learned from Eli, have you?"

"And my sister. She's on the SAR team."

"Kansas Colton. Stationed locally, right?"

"Yes."

"All right. Now, about the shooter—"

Spence nodded. "I never saw the guy, but Hetty got a glimpse of him right before he shot her. Probably why he shot her."

"We'll need to talk to Ms. Amos, of course—"

"When the doctors say you can," Spence said firmly.

The two men blinked. Exchanged glances. "Of course," Reynolds said.

Spence had the feeling they wouldn't stop short of applying a little pressure to those doctors if they felt they had to. So he'd just be darned sure he was around in case they tried.

"Any idea why he'd come after you? For that matter, which one was he after?"

"None. And he shot at both of us, as it happened. Maybe he just likes taking potshots at people. Or he decided that camp is his. Or that the whole hunting area is, and we trespassed. Or he hid something he didn't want found…"

His voice trailed off. He knew he had to tell them, and the sooner, the better, but that didn't make it any more pleasant. The two men waited, as if they sensed this would go more smoothly if they didn't push. He wasn't a suspect, after all.

"There's something else…" he began. "We found a body up there. One that's been there a while."

The two men went very still. "A body?"

Spence tried to remember the way both Eli and his sister talked about cases, when they did. Tried to give the kind of concise version they always managed.

"Appears to be a woman, long dark hair, mostly buried, but with her head and left arm above ground." He got out his phone and brought up the string of photos he'd taken.

He picked the one that best showed the position and condition of the body and showed it to them. They went very still.

"Arranged," the one in plain clothes murmured.

"What I thought," Spence agreed.

Dad had gone stiffly still beside him. Rigid, in fact. Belatedly, it hit him. He looked at his father apologetically. "Sorry, Dad. I didn't think about—"

Ryan Colton let out an audible breath. "It's all right, son. I just wasn't prepared for that."

The two cops were looking at Dad with interest. "It's ancient family history," Spence said quickly. "Almost thirty years ago ancient."

Both men nodded then and he wondered how much of the Colton history was common knowledge around here. He'd never wondered that before, and he felt rather guilty that he'd so successfully put it out of his mind. True, he hadn't even been born yet, but it had shaped his father and older cousin, and he should be more aware.

"Is this connected to the shooter you encountered?" asked Barton.

"No idea. Like I said, it looked like she'd been there a while."

"What's that on her hand?" Reynolds asked, peering closely at the image on the phone.

"A fake, I'd guess," said Barton. "Nobody'd leave a real diamond that size behind."

Spence hesitated then reached into his pocket and brought out the small bag with the ring they were staring at in the photo. "I know removing evidence isn't good, but there were signs of recent animal predation in the vicinity,

and I thought it would be better to have it than get there
and find it's vanished into some rodent den or something."

The two law enforcement men stared at the bag. Barton
reached out to take it, almost gingerly.

"I didn't touch it directly," Spence explained. "I used
some sterile gauze that was in that bag, and it went right
back in."

Because I used all the rest of that gauze on Hetty's leg.

"Look," he said abruptly, "I need to get back and see
how Hetty's doing. If you want to talk to me more, come
on inside."

"We'll need a formal statement from both of you," Barton said, then, rubbing at his jaw, changed it to, "Two formal statements from both you and Ms. Amos."

"Right now," Spence insisted, "I need a formal statement from the doctor, saying she's going to be all right."

He didn't get that when they first went inside. There was
no news yet, he was told, and to please take a seat. After a
brief conversation with the woman who appeared to be in
charge of the emergency intake, Barton led Spence over
to a private meeting room. He went, after his father nodded at him encouragingly, saying he'd stay right there and
interrupt with any word on Hetty.

The room was very small, a table with two chairs on
each side, and not much else. Except a painting on one
wall that looked to Spence to be of a spot along Thomp-
son Pass. A spot he'd been to a time or two, he thought as
he studied the piece. He wondered idly who had painted it
as he sat down.

It didn't hit him until the two other men sat across from
him that this was likely the private room where bad news

got passed along. He suppressed a shiver, thinking about people who had probably had their lives upended in this room with word that their loved one or family member had not made it.

He shook it off and looked at Reynolds and Barton.

"You want this in chronological order or order of importance?" Not to him, of course. To him, Hetty was the most important, but he'd been around Eli and Kansas enough to know what these guys would consider important.

"Let's start with the as-it-happened version," Barton said.

Spence walked them through it, from the engine shutting down, Hetty's skillful landing, them radioing for help, checking the area for any wildlife to be cautious around, setting up the campsite, even, embarrassedly, admitted he'd stupidly left his rifle in the storage shed, thinking he'd already checked for natural threats and he'd be right back anyway.

He'd never expected a human threat.

He went through the rest, ending with Dad's arrival, thinking that *We spent the night in the cave* was far too simple an explanation for what had really happened in those intervening hours.

"And you never saw the shooter?" Reynolds asked again.

"No. All I can tell you is what she told me." He went through Hetty's description of the man, including the possible scar that might not be a scar.

He didn't know how long they'd been sitting there, going over it again and yet again, before the door opened. Rapidly, without even a knock. His father was there, a look of pained worry on his face.

"Dad?" he asked, a little shakily as he got to his feet.

"She crashed, son. It's bad. They...don't know if she's going to make it."

Chapter 16

Spence didn't think he'd ever heard the term "traumatic shock" before, and he certainly had never heard of "hypovolemic shock." He had heard Dr. Masters say something about an overwhelming inflammatory response, in turn causing acute respiratory distress, and heard about the possibility of something called MODS—multiple organ dysfunction…syndrome, he thought—but he wasn't really processing all the words.

All he was certain of was the doctor's grim expression and the words, *It doesn't look good right now.*

Even the woman's assurance that if Spence hadn't done what he'd done so quickly, this could have happened out in the cave and he would have had only a body to bring home, didn't help much.

"But she was…fine. Hurting, but fine," he finally said, feeling more than a little lost. And a lot guilty. How could he have left Hetty and gone off with the cops while she'd been fighting for her life? It didn't matter that she'd seemed fine when she'd gone in, she'd been shot and he should have stayed with her.

How had he not realized how seriously injured she was?

How could he have just watched them wheel her away and then take off for essentially a chat in the park?

"It happens," Dr. Masters said. "Adrenaline and other reactions to being under stress, as you two obviously were, can keep someone going beyond what we'd expect. But then when the crash comes…" She hesitated. "We'll have to watch her very carefully. She's in serious condition, Mr. Colton. The next several hours are critical."

"Can I see her? I…need to see her."

"Not just yet. When we get her settled in ICU with all the monitors we need, we'll let you know."

It wasn't until the doctor walked away that Spence realized his father was staring at him. He must have sounded as desperate as he felt.

"I know going through something like this is…intense," Dad said very quietly. "But…is there something else going on here, Spence?"

Like what? That we both confessed during the night that we've always had feelings for each other? Since eleventh grade? And now she's in there fighting for her life. Should I have kept my stupid mouth shut? I should have—

His father's arm around his shoulders cut off the runaway train of thought. An image from long ago, when he'd been a kid, flashed through his mind, of his father explaining why the Colton family motto was Believe.

Your aunt Caroline deserved to be believed, Spence, and because she wasn't, she ended up murdered, along with our parents. A high price to pay for a lesson we'll never forget. If you have a problem, if something's wrong, tell us. If you can't tell me or your mom, tell your uncle or aunt. And do it knowing we will first and foremost believe you.

He could talk to Mom about it. Maybe not Dad, who seemed to be on a "When am I going to get grandchildren?" binge of late. And that was something Spence wasn't ready to deal with. He wasn't sure he ever would be. But then, he had been certain he could never be honest with Hetty, either, yet last night he had been.

He gave a shake of his head. It seemed much longer than mere hours since he'd finally admitted his feelings for Hetty.

He opened his mouth to speak but closed it again. They had been so wrapped up in the revelation that they'd both been hiding how they'd felt about each other for so long, they'd said nothing about where things would go from here. Nothing about future plans.

And now Hetty might not have a future.

"Later, Dad," he said finally. "When I'm sure she's going to be all right."

Because if she wasn't, there was no point. To anything.

"All right, son. Just know that we love you and whatever you decide, we're with you."

Spence wasn't sure he understood what his father meant, because there was no way he could know what had happened up in that cave. He shoved it aside for now, because only one thing mattered.

The ICU nurse was kind and gentle, but Spence suspected she could be tough as nails. He'd encountered the kind side first when she'd let him stay in the room with Hetty while she went about her business.

He found he could only watch Hetty for so long before he got twitchy because she wasn't moving. Hetty being still was a rare occurrence; she was always on the verge of motion. Seeing her lying motionless only pounded home to him how bad this really must be.

His mind was whirling as if it could make up for her stillness by racing in all directions at once. Was life really this unfair that it would take her away the moment they'd admitted the surface tension between them had always been just that, on the surface? That it had masked something else they'd both thought had to be kept hidden? So—what?— they realized it, admitted it, and then it was yanked away?

Or was it that they had to go through this? Was it that nothing less than some kind of near-death experience was what it took to blast through the decade-thick barrier they'd built between them, Spence mostly with flippancy, Hetty with biting sarcasm? Maybe it took this to shatter those two solid facades?

But why her? Why not him? Spencer wished it had been. Not because he thought he was tougher than she was—he wasn't at all sure of that—but because he hated to think of her in such pain. Hated to think of her hanging on the edge like this. He'd rather it was him than to be sitting there watching her like this.

He should have realized. He should have known how badly she was hurt, never mind that she'd kept saying she was all right. He should have known by the way she had opened up and talked, if nothing else. Hetty never did that. Not with him, anyway.

Had she known? Had she somehow realized this was going to turn bad on her? Was that why she'd opened up last night, why she'd admitted that he hadn't been the only one feeling attraction since all the way back in high school?

That idea jabbed at him worst of all. Why wouldn't she

have told him if she was feeling that bad? He would have figured out a way to get her out of there sooner if he'd known she was going to crash like this. Somehow. Even if he'd had to carry her every step of the way.

Spence would have sworn the clock over the door had somehow been piped through a loudspeaker because he could hear every ticked second as if it echoed off the walls. Every second that went by that she didn't move, didn't wake up. The nurse glanced at him now and then, smiling in understanding, and he wondered how she could stand this kind of work. People weren't nearly appreciative enough of individuals in this profession, until it came to hellish times like this.

He'd muted his phone an hour ago, when he'd first come in to sit at her bedside. Out of the need for distraction he pulled it out and saw a screen full of missed calls and texts. He knew Hetty's brother Troy was out on an oil rig so he wasn't surprised that there wasn't anything from him. Every other sibling she had, which meant five, had all texted. Then there was Dad, checking back in, and Mom, saying she'd be there in an hour. Hetty's mom, who was out of town, had left a voice message saying she was on her way back. His cousin Lakin, who was very close to Hetty, had also texted she was on her way.

And at the end of the list, a brief text from his cousin Eli, only saying he'd see him soon. So he probably had been assigned the case of the body they'd found. Something Spence was having a little trouble caring about at the moment.

A quiet whisper of his name came from the doorway and he looked up to see Parker standing there. He got up and walked over to him, and they stepped outside the room, although Spence made sure he was standing where he could still see her.

"How is she?"

"Not great." He couldn't help the grim tone in his voice.

"She's as tough as she needs to be, Spence. She'll pull through."

She has to. She just has to.

He didn't say it aloud, afraid it would come out as nothing less than a whine.

"Let me know if anything changes, will you?" Parker asked. "I'm going to head out with Chuck to see what can be done about the plane."

"Okay." Then, as his brain woke up to what his cousin had actually said—that he and the RTA mechanic were going to the campsite where it had all happened—he added sharply, "Hey, wait, we don't know if that guy is still out there."

Parker's mouth quirked. "Aw, cuz, you care."

Something hot and sharp welled up inside him. "Don't joke around when Hetty's lying in there possibly dying."

Parker looked startled then thoughtful. "Well, well," he murmured.

"What's that supposed to mean?"

"Nothing," his cousin said almost cheerfully. He turned to go then looked back. "Except it's about time."

Spence stared after his cousin. What was *that* supposed to mean? And when had that become the question of the day?

For a moment he just stood there, feeling a little stunned. Was he wearing a freaking sign or something? First Dad, hinting that he'd known something was brewing. Now

Parker, acting like he'd known all along that all the sniping and poking at each other was a cover.

He let out a compressed breath, shoved all that aside, too, and went back into the room where the only thing that really mattered right now lay so very, very still.

Chapter 17

Spence had lost track of who all had come and gone. He'd vacated his spot for Hetty's family, but not for just friends. All of the siblings except Troy had already been, he thought, but with seven total, he could be wrong. He hadn't had much, if any, sleep since things had gotten bad.

He was back in the almost-comfortable reclining chair next to her bed, dozing in and out, when he heard the nurse talking to someone fairly close by.

"—and he hasn't left her side since. It's actually very sweet," the nurse was saying to whoever it was.

He opened groggy eyes to look, and felt a jolt when he realized it was her mother. He swung his legs over and got to his feet, although it took him a moment to steady himself.

He was startled when the petite woman came straight to him and clasped both his hands in hers.

"Thank you, Spence."

He blinked. "For what?" *Taking her out where she got shot? For assuming she was going to be okay and deciding to stick the night out up there instead of carrying her down to somewhere Dad could have picked her up even at night?*

"For saving her and getting her here alive."

"Should have gotten her here sooner," he said gruffly, unable to meet her eyes.

"But the doctor said this didn't happen until after she was here. It's not your fault."

"It is. I'm the one who thought she'd be okay once the bleeding stopped. But she lost more than I realized and I—"

"Spence, stop. You're the one who stopped that bleeding, or she would have died out there. She wouldn't have even had the chance to fight."

He should have protested, should have explained exactly how he'd been stupid about it, not realizing how severely injured she'd actually been. But when Hetty's mother leaned up and planted a kiss on his cheek, he couldn't say a single word.

She then rushed over to Hetty's bedside, taking her daughter's hand in hers gently. He knew she was close to all her kids—all seven of them—but guessed there was a special, different kind of bond with the only girl. He remembered when Hetty's father, Charles Amos, had died of a fast-moving cancer. He had been an executive with an oil company where he had started out working the same job his son Troy now had on the oil rigs. His death had left Hetty's mother with seven kids to finish raising, but she'd never faltered.

He watched the two for a moment then realized he should probably leave them some privacy. He stepped out into the hallway and leaned wearily back against the wall. So wearily that the ICU nurse even paused to ask if he was all right.

"I'm all right as long as she is," he said with a nod toward the room behind him.

When Mrs. Amos came out some time later, he'd finally sat down on one of the benches outside Hetty's room. She took a seat beside him, reached out and laid a hand over his. He looked down at them, so tired, he caught himself comparing skin tone, how Hetty's was somewhere in between his and her mother's. But the green eyes? They were the forever gift from Charles Amos, and he wondered what it was like to see that both loving and painful reminder every time you looked in a mirror.

When Mrs. Amos spoke, it was with quiet certainty. "That old saying about hindsight being twenty-twenty is true, you know. You had no way of knowing this could happen. The blame lies squarely on the predator who did this, not you."

"I still should have—"

He stopped when her mother shook her head. Because you just didn't argue with this matriarch. "No. You did everything you could and should have. And you've stayed with her, by her side, through it all. My only girl, our treasure, has a chance, thanks to you, and your father." She paused then gave Spence an odd sort of smile. "You've been a big part of her life for so long, I'm not surprised you'd be the one to help her through this."

When she'd gone back to her daughter, Spence sat running those last words through his weary mind over and over again, wondering if there was some deeper meaning there.

He should leave, he belatedly realized. Her mother was there now, she didn't need him. And when she had needed him, he'd completely missed how bad things really were and she'd nearly died because of it. Because, when they'd been huddled under that survival blanket last night, all he could think of was her, how good she felt and how much better he felt after finally letting out the secret he'd carried all these years.

And how amazing it had felt to hear her admit to pretty much the same thing. All those times when she'd jabbed at him, when she'd sniped at him, it had been for the same reason he'd always flirted with clients or other women in front of her; to hide the truth. They'd been playing this silly game, each of them hiding their feelings behind differing masks, until fate had stepped in and slapped them both upside the head.

"Wake up, Hetty," he whispered to the momentarily empty hallway. "You've got to wake up."

When Hetty first heard the low hum of…something, she thought… She wasn't sure what she thought. It didn't sound like her plane, and she wouldn't have been sleeping if it was. But then she remembered that jolt of adrenaline when the engine had died…then the shots. The searing agony of the bullet tearing through her flesh. Her next thought was that she had died and this was what it smelled like. That startled her into opening her eyes.

She had to blink several times against the unexpected brightness. She had the fleeting notion that this was some kind of waiting room where you went after you died. Or maybe when you were in the process of dying.

But then there was movement and a moment later she was looking up into Spence's face. Still groggy, she was struck with the horrible fear that he was dead, too. Had the shooter gotten him? Had he been hurt and she hadn't known? Her pulse kicked up and suddenly she was a bit more awake.

"Hey," he whispered. "Welcome back."

"I...what? Where?"

"Easy," Spence said soothingly. "We're in Wasilla. Do you remember my dad coming for us?"

"I..." She scrunched her eyes closed then opened them again, determinedly shoving back at that groggy feeling. "Yes," she said.

And she did remember lying across the back seats of the RTA helo, held in place by seat belts. Looking up at the sky as they'd wheeled her into the emergency room. Most of all, she remembered the look on Spence's face when they'd gone through those swinging doors, leaving him on the other side. And that was about the last thing she remembered.

The rest, the before part, came back to her in a rush now: last night huddled in the cave, the things they'd said, the things they'd finally admitted. She would have probably felt her cheeks heat if another question hadn't arisen almost immediately.

"How long?"

"You've been pretty out of it for almost twenty-four hours. It's Tuesday morning."

She frowned. "Why? Did they drug me? I wasn't feeling that bad, did they have to—"

She stopped abruptly when Spence reached out and cupped her cheek. Yesterday—no, two days ago apparently—that would have been unthinkable. Now, it was... She wasn't sure what it was. Other than it felt good.

As she lay there looking up at him, she saw an odd sheen

in his deep blue eyes. Tears? Why on earth would Spence Colton be tearing up?

He reached down and pressed a button on a cord that ran along the bed rail before he looked at her and said, "You crashed, Hetty. Pretty hard. Traumatic shock, they called it. From what they said, I guess once the adrenaline ebbed away, once you didn't have to fight anymore, your body finally realized you weren't doing so great."

"Oh."

She didn't know what else to say. So she simply looked at Spence's handsome face and, for the first time since they'd been kids, allowed herself to truly appreciate his good looks. Looks she had always had to pretend to assess scornfully as the major tool he used to entrance clients.

Words came back to her then, in his voice, as he'd said them that night in the cave.

The looks were just part of the act, part of the cocky wise-ass routine that kept people from seeing the real me. The stupid me I always thought I was until you showed me another way.

She had never realized he'd thought himself stupid. Perhaps because she knew better, because she'd dealt with that agile mind so closely during those tutoring sessions. She'd seen the quickness of his thinking, the way he solved puzzles, the way complex mathematical problems never fazed him, the way he designed things that would actually work simply because he liked doing it.

Anything that didn't involve traditional reading, he whizzed through. This was far from the first time that she was grateful for the study she'd read that had suggested a way to use that visual acuity of his, that design ability, and relate it to the kind of language and writing the majority of the world used.

The memory that shot into her mind then was the day he'd come back for a session after they'd started using that technique and thrown his arms around her in a thank-you that was nothing less than joyous. Maybe because that was the way he was looking at her now. And that alone told her how serious these last hours she wasn't even aware of must have been.

"Thank you for getting me out of there," she said, aware her throat was a little sore and wondering if she'd had some kind of tube rammed down her throat at some point. She'd ask, later. The doctor, she decided, since she didn't really want Spence to have to tell her about the worst of it.

"Thank Dad, he did the flying."

"But you did the heavy lifting," she said, wishing now she hadn't been hurting quite so much so she could remember better how it had felt to have this man carrying her. But all she remembered was how steady his pace had been, how careful he'd been not to jostle her, how he'd held her as if she were some precious thing he hadn't dared drop.

"You're not heavy." A flash of the old Spence grin warmed her. "It's just all that muscle, girl."

A woman in scrubs came in, quickly rushing to her bedside, saying how glad she was to see her awake. Spence started to move aside, and instinctively Hetty grabbed his hand. She didn't want him to go.

"She needs to check some things," he said soothingly. "And I need to call your mom. She went to get some rest. And text Troy. And the rest of your family, who've all been here, several times. My family, too. Everybody was worried."

She nodded, feeling a little tired as it started to register just how bad it must have been, to pull everyone here. It might only be a hundred and ten miles as the helicopter flew from Shelby to Wasilla, but it was about two and a half times that if you tried to drive. And her mother had been in Seattle with friends, taking a well-earned and long-delayed vacation.

She watched him go, phone in hand, as he left the room.

"That boy," the woman beside her said with a smile as she made notes from the monitor readings at the head of the bed, "has not left your side since you were moved in here. He gave your mom some space, but nobody else. He was a better guard dog than my German shepherd. He must love you a lot."

Hetty felt her pulse leap at those last words, and the nurse laughed as it registered on the monitor.

"He'd kick-start my pulse, too, honey, but he's only got eyes for you."

No matter how the woman poked and prodded, Hetty didn't feel much of anything after that.

Chapter 18

Hetty didn't realize she'd dozed off again—which was irritating in itself, since she had been lying there for a day and a half and thought she should be feeling better—until she opened her eyes to see Lakin Colton standing there. The woman who was the office manager at RTA and also her brother Troy's girlfriend since elementary school, was looking down at her with obvious worry in her warm brown eyes.

"Hi," she said with the best reassuring smile she could manage. She realized she was feeling a bit better, so she had to reluctantly admit that the sleep Spence had kept urging her to get was doing some good.

"I've been so horribly worried," Lakin admitted. "I was afraid we were going to lose you."

"I'm too stubborn," Hetty said, keeping that smile going.

"I'm glad," the younger woman said. "I'd be lost without you. We girls are outnumbered at RTA. All those Colton boys."

Yes, those Colton boys. Hetty had to hide her reaction to the observation. Until she and Spence had a chance to talk about the changes that had—she hoped—happened that night in the cave, she didn't want to sharpen the already-too-perceptive gazes of said Colton males by saying anything that would start them prodding Spence for answers.

"Four of them, three of us counting Kansas," Hetty said. "That makes us pretty much even."

Lakin was smiling now. "You would know. You're the one girl among six Amos boys, and you still rule."

Hetty laughed at that. She held her own as the middle child of seven and the only girl, but rule? She didn't think so. "They might dispute that."

"Troy wouldn't. He was really worried about you, too. I've never heard him so upset about being stuck out on the rig."

"Well, he should be more upset about leaving you alone for months at a time," Hetty said firmly.

Lakin might be reluctant to criticize him, but Troy was Hetty's little brother—well, the first of the three younger ones anyway, which balanced out the three older ones—and she had the right and felt no hesitation. She knew Lakin loved Troy, and thought that he really did love her back, but if he didn't start getting his head in the game and paying more attention to her rather than assuming she would always be there waiting, he was going to blow it.

Funny how easy it was to fix her brother's situation, but how long it had taken to address hers with Spence. Assuming, of course, that they had. He'd been reluctant to talk about it while she was in here, and she understood because there was always somebody around, hovering, and she didn't like the idea of strangers listening in on that particular discussion, either. Or family, for that matter. At least not until they'd worked it all out between themselves.

Although she had to admit she was starting to wonder if

maybe she'd jumped the gun a little. Maybe that night had been a moment of weakness Spence regretted now. Maybe he wanted to go back to their old, sparring ways, keeping some distance between them at all times.

Lakin looked a little embarrassed at her words and Hetty wondered if it was because she'd had a similar thought. "I don't want you two breaking up," she said firmly. "I've got my heart set on having you as a sister, Lakin Colton."

"I'd like that," Lakin said almost shyly. "I love my family, but I love yours, too. And I'd like to see us all…connected, you know?"

"Now that," Hetty said, thinking of the seven Amos siblings related to the four Coltons, "would be an amazing family."

After Lakin left a little while later, Hetty thought she would love to see this woman who was a dear friend have that kind of combined family behind her. She was aware of the fact that Lakin, abandoned by her biological parents, had been left at a local grocery store.

She'd been given to a foster family, but when Sasha Colton, Will's wife, had encountered her, she had instantly fallen for the bright-eyed, intelligent child. They'd taken her in, and all three of the Colton boys had promptly followed suit, doting on the endearing, smart newcomer who'd quickly returned the favor by adoring her new big brothers. Hetty suspected that Lakin barely even remembered she wasn't a Colton by birth, and that the rest of the Coltons rarely thought of it, either.

The rest of us just got born. You got chosen.

Hetty remembered Lakin telling her about those words, spoken to her at a young age by her ten-years-older brother

Eli. Words that had made her feel so special that she had let down the last of her barriers and fully become a Colton.

Become a Colton.

Sometimes Hetty felt like one simply because she was an integral part of RTA, but also because the entire Colton family, from Will and Sasha and Ryan and Abby to all the cousins, had made her feel that way. They were a tightly knit bunch, in some ways tighter than her own spread-out clan.

And now I know why.

The story Spence had told her of the slaughter of his aunt and grandparents had chilled her beyond even the worst Alaskan weather. She couldn't imagine having to deal with something like that. Even though Spence hadn't yet been born, it had to have affected him indirectly given the devastation it had wrought on his family.

And that story had made her appreciate the senior Coltons even more than she already had, simply because of the courage it had taken to relocate and build the entirely new and different and rock-solid life they had. Which included her, since she had the life she had—the life doing what she loved most—because of them, because they'd been willing to take a chance on a young inexperienced pilot.

She had, in part, Lakin to thank for that, for she knew her friend had pushed Will to take that chance. Which had made her, in turn, utterly determined to make sure they didn't regret it.

You could have really crashed.

With Hetty flying? Not a chance.

She doubted Spence and his dad realized she'd heard

them. But she had, and it had done more to ease her nerves than anything short of knowing rescue had arrived.

And that Spence had said it was the most soothing balm of all.

There weren't many men who could make Spence feel undersized, but his cousin Eli was one of them. He didn't know if it was that the guy was a couple of inches taller than his own six feet, that he was so strong and broad-shouldered, or simply that air of authority he carried around. With good reason, given his position in the Alaska Bureau of Investigation's Major Crimes Unit.

"Landed the case, huh?" he asked when he first saw Eli in the hospital hallway.

"Never mind that yet," Eli said, his eyes warm with obvious genuine concern. "How's Hetty?"

Points for that, cuz. Eli wasn't part of RTA, and although they'd never discussed it, Spence suspected the fact that he'd been with his father when they'd found the body of Caroline Colton and her killer had shaped his future. But that didn't mean his cousin didn't care about the family business, and he knew Hetty.

"She's going to be okay," he said firmly, as if the more confidently he said it would make it true. Although now, three days after those doors had swung shut on him and they'd taken her away, he really did believe it. She'd stabilized, they told him, and would be moving out of the ICU this afternoon. "They're going to move her into a regular room later today."

Eli let out a long breath then nodded. "Good." Then, visibly, he settled into business. "Thanks for thinking to take those pictures. And even though our lab guys are finicky and don't like anybody touching their evidence, I think you made the right call on the ring. I've been up there now, and the scene has already changed a little, likely from those animals you recognized were around."

Spence grimaced. The image of the dead woman was going to be one he'd probably carry forever. "Any idea who she...was?"

"Not yet. We're checking missing persons' reports, but no hits so far, and we can't assume she was a local."

"But it was a murder." He didn't really have any doubts, but he needed to hear it from the man who would know.

"Not much doubt about that. They've moved the body to the forensics lab. Montgomery jumped at the case, and he's good. Even if he does have a thing for your sister."

Spence blinked. "Scott's got a thing for Kansas?"

"Definitely." Eli grinned. "And it pays off for me, because if I need something in a hurry or after hours, he's always willing. Anyway, they're running DNA, but no definitive results yet."

Eli shifted subjects, a signal Spence recognized as meaning he'd shared all he could on the body they'd found.

"Locals have any idea on the shooter?"

Spence shook his head. "Theories range from some hunter who misfired but knew Hetty saw him so decided to take us out to just some random nutcase."

"Nothing connected to the clients who canceled?"

Spence blinked. That, he had to admit, had not occurred to him. Leave it to Eli. "I...don't know. I don't know if they've even considered that yet."

Eli gave a one-shouldered shrug. "Just a thought."

"I'll ask."

Could it be? Could the shooter have maybe been after the newlyweds, and shot at them by mistake, not knowing the Greshams had canceled at the last minute? Had this not been some random hunter run amok, but a…a hitman or something? Surely, he'd have known what his targets looked like. Or had he just assumed, at that distance, and based on location? But then, how had he even known where they were going?

So many questions tumbled through Spence's mind, it was a little dizzying. And he found himself staring at his cousin.

"What?" Eli asked.

"How do you…do it? What you do, I mean?" He realized when he said it that Eli might think he meant the kind of work he did, especially after being there when their aunt had been found. So he quickly added, "Start at the end and work back, I mean, when there are so many directions it could go in?"

Eli smiled widely. "Leave it to you to put it in a nutshell. That's exactly what it is, a lot of the time. Start with the results of the crime and work backward. And yeah, it means a lot of dead ends sometimes." Another shrug, as if it were nothing instead of a crucial part of civilized life. "Process of elimination."

"I'm glad we have people like you out there," Spence said, meaning it.

But that was not what lingered in Spence's mind after his cousin had left. It was the idea that both terrified and thrilled him at the same time.

The idea that he and Hetty might have been mistaken for newlyweds.

Chapter 19

"When do I get out of here?"

Hetty didn't mean to sound sharp, but she was about out of patience. She hated being cooped up here, hated the constant interruptions as someone checked on her, or made noise as they checked on someone else, or any of the other multitude of interruptions. She'd been spoiled, used to being in control, used to her quiet environment at home. The move out of the ICU was an improvement on a couple of fronts, noise among them, but she still wanted out as soon as possible.

The only good thing about this whole mess was Spence. He seemed to spend more time here than not, even though she knew there were clients booked for the rest of the summer. *Clients*, she thought with a sour twist of her mouth, *she should be flying*.

And that was the thought at the top of her mind when Spence came back into the room.

"Do they know what happened with the plane?" she demanded before anything else. He had told her his dad and Chuck were practically taking the thing apart to find out what had happened.

He didn't look startled at the abrupt question, or the lack

of greeting. She wondered if that was because she got like that when she was intent on something and he was used to it. She had a temper, she knew, and after three days in this place, it was a bit close to the surface.

No, he didn't look startled, but he did look a bit uncomfortable. "Spence?"

He let out an audible breath and said, in a tone so neutral it had to be intentional, "They have an idea, but it's not confirmed yet."

"I'm already tired of that phrase, whether it's about the plane, the shooter or when I'm getting out of here."

"You've always been a yes-or-no kind of person," Spence said dryly.

"If that means I don't take well to stalling, then yes."

"In this case, it's simple truth. They're looking at everything, and that takes time. And that," he added with that upward quirk of his mouth that used to irritate her but now seemed…charming, "applies to all three of your questions."

She made a face at him, one that had always made him laugh back in school, because she didn't want him to think she was upset with him rather than just the circumstances. All of them. She thought she saw him smother a laugh.

"I did talk to Eli, though," he said.

That caught her attention. "You did?"

He nodded. "He stopped by to see how you were. Your brothers were still here, so he said to just tell you hello and to get out of here soon."

"Well, I'm with him on that," she said the words heartfelt. "But does that mean he did get assigned to investigate…the body?"

Spence nodded. "They haven't identified her, or the manner of death yet. They moved the body to their lab and will have one of their best people working on it."

"But she was murdered, right? The way she was…arranged…" She suppressed a shudder.

"He thinks so."

She had the feeling there was something more, something he wasn't saying, but if it was something Eli had told him to keep in confidence, that was what he would do. Spence Colton was a man of his word. He would never break a promise. Or a vow—

Her thought was abruptly cut off when two people came through the door. Not hospital staff, as she would have expected, but two people she didn't recognize, at least until Spence greeted the first one in, a man in a pair of khaki pants and a casual jacket over a dress shirt. When she heard his voice, she realized he was the detective who had questioned her right after she'd awakened, the one who was working the case of their shooter. She'd still been a bit foggy then, so it took her a moment to place him.

A rather shy-looking woman in a pair of baggy jeans and a loose, flowing blouse in an almost Hawaiian print followed him in. She carried a small case of some kind, but the sketchpad in her other hand told Hetty why she was there. Spence had mentioned they wanted to try to do a sketch of the man she'd glimpsed, and had promised they understood it had only been a glimpse and at some distance.

"We usually do this at the station," Detective Barton said. "We've got a computer that does it, but frankly, I think Amy here is better."

The woman smiled. "Sometimes humans are better at

humans." Then, to Hetty, she said, "I'm glad you're feeling well enough to do this now."

"So am I," she said fervently.

Hetty found herself oddly distracted after Spence had bowed out and left the room, and had to make herself focus on the task. She had been sure this would be pointless, but the artist asked some either/or questions that had her realizing she might have noticed more than she'd thought.

After the artist had finalized the sketch, and Hetty had said that was the best she could do—it didn't look like anybody she'd recognize if she saw him again, but the hair was right—Detective Barton asked her some other questions, mostly about the weapon the man had used.

"We know the caliber fit a 6.5mm Creedmoor from the rounds we recovered at the site…" he began.

That surprised her. She hadn't realized they'd gone back there already. But then, she'd barely realized how much time had passed, she'd been so completely out of it. He went on.

"That's a common sniper round. Causes less recoil, and the trajectory—" He cut himself off. "Sorry, that's not what you need to think about. Think about the weapon itself."

She closed her eyes for a moment, trying to replay that moment in her mind. "All I know is it looked all black. Not a wood stock. And it had some kind of optical sight. But that's all I could see."

Barton nodded. "All right."

"You're sure he's gone?"

The man nodded. "We did a full sweep of the area before we went in to gather evidence."

"One round hit the plane," she said. "He almost hit

Spence." Just saying it gave her a little chill. And not just because if he'd also been hurt, they both could well have died out there.

The man nodded. "Your partner told us about that one, so we got that." *Your partner...* She wasn't sure how she felt about that term. "Guy did a number on the electronics there, didn't he."

It wasn't really a question, so she only nodded. She wondered how they were going to get the plane back from the lake. Wondered why there had been a problem in the first place.

"But that was after. It doesn't explain what happened to make the engine quit in the first place."

The detective grimaced. "It appears the fuel pump was tampered with."

Her brow creased. "The fuel pump? But that wouldn't kill the engine, not in that plane."

"So I was told, by your partner." *That word again.* "He said the pump is only for extra juice on takeoff, landing, and pushing for altitude, because of the location of the fuel tanks, in the wings."

Hetty nodded. "It's a high-wing plane, the fuel is gravity fed."

"Apparently our suspect didn't realize that, any more than I did," Barton said rather ruefully. "But the theory is whatever he did to mess with the pump eventually shifted and blocked the fuel line."

A sudden memory shot into her mind and her pulse kicked up. "You need to go talk to Jake, the teenager who works down at the RTA dock. He mentioned right before we left that there had been some guy down looking at the plane."

The detective went still. "Did he now," he said quietly, obviously seizing on the idea.

"He thought it was just some curious tourist," Hetty explained. "And all my preflight checks were fine, so I didn't think anything more about it."

"We'll get right on that," Barton assured her. "Anything else?"

"I don't think so," Hetty said, feeling as if she had scraped the very bottom of her memory bank.

"All right. Thank you."

He turned to the artist, who nodded to indicate she was done. And as he moved, his jacket slid back enough for Hetty to see the sidearm he wore on his belt. And suddenly something else floated up from that bottom. A brief but vivid flash of memory. And she felt she needed to say it, even if it might be pointless.

"I don't know if this means anything, I'm not that experienced with weapons, but..."

"Go ahead, please," Barton said.

"When I saw him, he was holding the rifle in his left hand."

Again the man went still. And then he smiled at her. "Well, now, that may just turn out to be very helpful. Get well, Ms. Amos."

"Working on it," she said, feeling quietly pleased that she might have actually helped to find the man who had put her here in this hospital bed.

Chapter 20

Spence was yawning as he stepped outside, but it cut off with an awkward cough when he realized he'd almost walked into his father's fist, raised to knock on his door.

He'd come home for a shower, a change of clothes, had almost dived into his bed for a nap, but told himself the shut-eye he'd caught in the reclining chair at Hetty's bedside would have to be enough. He needed to get back there. He didn't like being gone even this long. He'd only left because she'd had a physical therapy session. She was working hard at getting back on her feet, but she was going to be needing those crutches they'd given her for a while, no matter how much she obviously hated them.

Belatedly, he realized his father was holding out a bright blue mug with the familiar Roaster's logo. The café down on Main Street had the best coffee around, probably because it roasted its own beans. It was a standing joke among the locals of Shelby that you could always tell a tourist because they were drinking from one of the Roaster's paper cups instead of the refillable mugs all the regulars had.

But right now, all Spence cared about was the smell of that coffee and the caffeine jolt it promised. He grabbed it gratefully and his father let him take a long sip before he said, "We need to talk."

There was a grim undertone to the voice and Spence wondered if he had enough energy left to brace himself for whatever was coming. He stood aside for his dad to enter and they walked over to sit at the small dining table he rarely used. He waited. When his father didn't speak, he finally gave him a wry one-sided smile and said, "Just hit me with it, Dad."

Ryan Colton nodded. "All right. Two things. Chuck says there was a partial cut of the line to the fuel pump, which is why it only gave out when it tried to turn on for the controlled landing. And a piece that was cut off the line, he thinks maybe accidentally since it was just floating loose, blocked the fuel intake from the wing tanks."

That made sense, to him anyway. Hetty would be the one to really ask, but he didn't want her getting all wound up about that yet. Time enough when she was well enough to be released from the hospital.

"And second," Dad went on, "there may be a connection between RTA and your shooter."

Spence blinked. He remembered Eli's question and wondered at the instincts his cousin had developed that got him places long before anyone else. "What connection?"

"It's not certain, just a possibility," Dad cautioned. "In fact, it's a pretty slim possibility."

"Nothing in the last four—no, five—days has been certain," he said, his tone a little sour. "Just tell me."

"Well, you can thank your sister for this one…" his father began.

Spence drew back slightly. "Kansas?" Search and rescue was her bailiwick, and she was one of the best at it, but why would she have gotten involved with this, after the fact? "What did she find?"

A brief smile flashed across his father's face. "This time it's not what she found, it's what she thought of. Something no one else did. She called a friend of hers who's a cop in Portland."

Portland. Where the newlyweds who had canceled were from. So, both his sister and Eli had made the mental jump. He supposed that's what happened when you were in their line of work, your mind naturally went there.

"She'd be here to tell you herself but she got a call on a job over in Chugach," Dad went on, referring to the state park just down and across the sound from them. "Anyway, it turns out the new hubby's ex-wife is quite the piece of work. She's well known to the officers assigned to the district your couple lives in. Several domestic incidents with her on file."

That threw a whole different light on things. He frowned. "Hetty's positive the shooter was a guy, and I don't think she'd misjudge that. Which would mean…what?"

Dad gave a single-shouldered shrug and a shake of his head. "No idea. Friend? Relative?"

"Or…she hired someone," Spence said, feeling a little silly even saying it. Who on earth would hire a…a hitman to try and take out your ex? *A lot of people. You know that.*

"That did occur to me," Dad said grimly.

The pieces were tumbling around in his head. "But why would he come after us if the ex is the target? Not like he could mistake us for them. And is the guy who tampered with the plane also the shooter? Did he follow us out there? How else could he even have known where we were going?"

"Slow down there, son. One step at a time. How long were you there before it all started?"

"A couple of hours, maybe."

"Enough time for somebody to get there," Dad said. "But that'd pretty much mean it has to be a local, because some guy from Portland isn't going to be able to just find his way out there."

"Unless he hired somebody to take him there," Spence said.

"Good point," Dad admitted. "I think I'll head down to the marina and ask around a bit before I get you back to Wasilla. Maybe I can find something."

"Aren't the cops supposed to be doing that?" Spence asked, grateful that he didn't have to explain to his father than he had to get back to Hetty. That he was already restless and nervous being away from her.

"There's only so many of them," Dad said. "Shelby PD is small, and you know how strapped Bobby Reynolds always says they are. Besides, this is kind of a wild hair that might well be a dead end."

"Yeah," Spence agreed, even though his brain was latching onto the idea as the most logical. It made more sense to him than some random guy out there just taking it in his head to shoot at a couple of total strangers.

But if it was true, what did it mean? That he didn't know what his targets looked like and thought they were the couple? He and Hetty?

If only.

Spence mentally stomped on the urge to pour out what

had happened up in the cave that night to his dad. He wasn't ready for that, wouldn't be until he and Hetty had a chance to talk without family, friends and an entire medical staff lurking about. But setting that aside—which took more of an effort than he was used to—and after Dad had left to head down to the marina, he thought it through.

The ex hired a guy. If she'd somehow found a local, that answered the next few questions. Otherwise, she'd hired someone from Portland who'd came up here. Either the woman had to have known her ex had booked with RTA, or maybe the hitman had found out somehow. It wasn't like they'd kept everything secret. In fact, Lakin, in all her cleverness, had arranged some newlywed-type trappings from local suppliers for the trip, so it could easily have gotten out that they'd had a booking of that kind.

So, he tried tampering with the plane, but didn't know enough about them to realize that a broken fuel pump wouldn't bring down a gravity-fed system. And what? Got lucky that he had managed to do some damage that later did bring it down, as things had shifted during the flight?

He pushed that aside and went back to visualizing the plan. So, the plane was not supposed to land safely—*Didn't count on Hetty being as good as she is, did you, jackass?*—and the guy went to their destination just to be sure it didn't? To make sure he'd completed the job? How, by searching the wreckage for bodies? Or if his sabotage effort had worked, would he have just assumed when they hadn't arrived that it was mission accomplished, that they were down in deep water and beyond help or rescue?

And then what? He sees the plane land safely—thanks to its stellar pilot—but then realizes his quarry was never

aboard and...what? Panics? Decides he has to kill them anyway? Or maybe he had just been trying to drive them away
so he could escape unseen. That made more sense. Except,
Hetty had seen him, which had changed everything. He
wouldn't want to leave a witness behind, so he'd started to
hunt her, and Spence because he was with her. Was that it?

He gave a sharp shake of his head. It was crazy. The
whole freaking thing was crazy. The only thing he was really sure of was that the shooter knew Hetty had seen him,
which was why he'd tried to take her out so many times.
And had come too damned close to succeeding.

Frankly, for him, that was all the certainty he needed.
And as soon as Hetty was well enough, he was going to
see to it that the guy never had a chance to try again, if he
had to go out there and hunt him down himself.

Spence suddenly understood how his parents and his
aunt and uncle had found the courage to leave everything
they'd known behind and move here to Alaska, changing their lives in so many ways. Because this had already
changed him, somewhere deep inside. Between finding
that half-buried body and nearly losing the woman he'd
finally admitted he cared so much for, he was feeling a bit
beyond fierce.

He'd never hunted a man before. But all it took was the
image of Hetty hooked up to every medical machine he
could imagine, barely clinging to life, to convince him that
he not only could but would.

Chapter 21

Hetty was certain that if she didn't get out of here soon she was going to explode. This was day five of her stay and she'd had enough. She was surprised her blood pressure wasn't through the roof every time they came in and wrapped the cuff around her arm. It was in no small part because she knew Spence had put everything on hold to be with her. To be with her practically every moment she was awake. And, judging by the times she'd awakened in the dark—they used blackout curtains to simulate actual darkness at night in the hospital—most of the time when she was sleeping, too.

Which meant RTA had to be scrambling, minus their premier guide who had been booked solid all month, and down a pilot. This had to have thrown them into complete chaos. If only she'd noticed that guy sooner. If only she'd realized something was wrong with the plane. If only, if only, if only...

But on second thought, she wasn't sure she'd trade that night in the cave with Spence, when the truth between them had finally come out into the open, for anything.

Even for not being shot.

She wrapped her arms around herself. She was anxious

to talk to him, really talk, without anybody else around to interrupt. But she had no idea when that might happen. She had sent her mother back to finish her vacation, insisting it was the first real break she'd taken in years, and that she would be fine. She'd told her brothers to back off; that she needed to concentrate on recuperation and didn't need them dropping in five times a day. She'd even—with ulterior motive—told Troy that if he wanted to call multiple times a day to see how she was to call Lakin instead, so she could focus on healing.

She did not, however, tell Spence to back off. She couldn't bring herself to do it, not when she got so much quiet pleasure out of waking up and seeing him there, so close at hand, or when she thought he'd finally left but then he strolled in the door a few minutes later.

Hetty pushed herself extra hard at therapy that morning, both to vent her frustration and because the harder she worked at it, the sooner she'd get out of here. She was exhausted after the hour and a half session, which alone told her how much farther she had to go. At one time, she could have done everything the therapist asked her to without even breathing faster. Now, it was an effort unlike anything she'd had to make before, except for that night at the lake when she'd been in such pain from the gunshot wound. And even then, once Spence had found her, she hadn't had to do much, since he had carried her. Carried her with such ease, such care, such…tenderness.

But she would make the effort. Every day if she had to. She had learned to handle the crutches, although she didn't like it. If they would get her out of this place, she'd deal. Although now she was almost tired enough for a nap. But no sooner was she back sitting on the edge of the bed in her room, pondering if she dared try lifting her injured leg up under its own power or if she should use her hands to maneuver it, than the door opened.

She sucked in a breath and tried to paste on her cheerful face, something else she'd adopted in her effort to escape. But when she turned to look, she was sure the expression had frozen.

It was Spence. And he was pushing an empty wheelchair. Well, empty except for a small duffel bag on the seat. And with him were his parents. Ryan and Abby Colton were smiling widely. And, in their case, it was for real, unlike the effort she'd made. Abby's smile in particular was warm, and her short, bouncy bob suited her so well. Her eyes were green, although a different shade than her own, and they were actually sparkling, as if she was delighted to be there.

"You ready to get out of here?" Ryan—she always had trouble even thinking of him by his first name, no matter his insistence, because he was, in essence, her boss—asked, his smile becoming a grin.

"Out?" She almost yelped. "Seriously?"

"Well, it'd be a pretty lousy prank if we weren't," drawled Spence.

"And we need to hurry before I get accused of bribing a source on the biggest story this town has had in years," said an also grinning Abby, obviously referring to her job as a reporter for the local newspaper, the *Shelby Weekly*.

Hetty winced inwardly at the reminder of not only the man who had shot her, but the body they'd found, but she selfishly let the personal news outweigh it. She was getting out.

"I don't need the chair, really," she said, experiencing a burst of energy that made her feel as if she'd already healed.

"You don't," Spence agreed easily, "but the hospital requires it." He flashed his own grin at her, which somehow had a lot more impact. "How about we let you climb into the bird on your own?"

She blinked. "You flew here?"

"So I'm impatient," Spence quipped.

"Besides," his father said, "I think that drive in a car would be a little much for you right now." His mouth quirked. "And for me, for that matter. I'm spoiled, I much prefer flying."

They all seemed so happy, as if they were rescuing one of their own. They had always said she was family, and had always treated her that way, but if she had any doubts left that they really meant it, they were vanquished by the happiness that now filled the room. And she found herself grinning right back at them, the unexpected gift of freedom too much to hold in.

"Now, you're still under doctor's orders," Abby said in the same kind of tone her mother used when she was giving instructions to one of her brood. "So you have to take it easy."

"And we'll enforce that, if necessary," Ryan said. "We have your room ready and waiting—"

"My room?" Hetty said, staring at Spence's dad.

Abby laughed. "Leave it to him to put the end of the story first. You're staying with us, dear."

"But—"

Abby hushed her with a wave. "Not up for negotiation. The only reason they agreed to release you was our promise that you'd be in a place with no stairs. So, your upstairs apartment does not cut it. Now, I talked with your friend Dove, and she told me what clothes she thought would work, and told us where the extra key was hidden, so we went and gathered those for you," she said, indicating the bag on the wheelchair seat.

Redheaded Dove St. James ran Namaste, the small yoga studio on Main Street in town, a place Hetty frequented when she needed some calm. So, often. Often enough that she and Dove had become good friends. And since her studio was right down the street from Hetty's apartment, it was a handy spot to stash a backup key to her place.

"She'll also look into some special techniques that might be helpful, when the doctor says you're ready," Abby went on, leaving Hetty feeling like her head was spinning a little. All the things she'd been trying to figure out—including how she was going to manage the stairs to her apartment—seemed to have magically been solved.

"Wow," she said. "Got a problem, turn the Coltons loose on it."

They all laughed, and she knew she'd found the right words to thank them. Spence had stayed mostly quiet since his first wisecrack, but Hetty had the feeling that if she dug down deep enough, she'd find that he had started this.

"Absolutely," agreed Ryan. Then, his tone suddenly solemn, he added, "After all, RTA got you into this fix. You wouldn't have been up there if you weren't working for us."

"And you'll be needing somebody around in case you need help with something," Abby continued. "You'll need to keep your leg elevated, the dressings changed and probably ice packs for any swelling at first. I've arranged to work from home for the next couple of weeks, so we're all set. And your mother can enjoy her vacation without worrying that you're alone while you're healing."

Hetty sat silently for a moment, staring at this couple she'd always admired. She didn't know what to say. She truly had been worried that her mother might cancel this first vacation she'd taken in years, to rush home and take care of her. She'd almost done it when she'd first arrived at the hospital, but Hetty had convinced her to go back to her plans and that she would call her if she needed help.

And now she had all the help she could possibly need, and she hadn't even had to ask.

Because Spence had asked for her. She was sure of that now. And his family had come through, like they always did.

She remembered what he'd told her that night in the cave; the horrible story of the murders of the aunt and grandparents he'd never known. Whether that was the genesis of the Colton trait of helping whoever needed it or not, she didn't know, but if she had to guess, she would say it probably was. And this time she was the lucky recipient.

On some level beneath the joy, she registered the discomfort as Abby helped her get dressed in the comfortable and thankfully easy-to-put-on clothes they'd brought, and was almost glad to sit in the wheelchair when it was done. Abby also kept talking and, by the way Spence's mother kept glancing at her, Hetty knew it was to distract her from the pain.

"You'll have to sign some papers at the desk on the way out, but Spence gave them all the info so you won't have to spend an hour filling out the rest of the forms," she was saying.

For the first time since he'd cracked the joke about flying here to get her because he was impatient, she looked up at Spence.

"Thank you," she said vehemently, hoping he understood she meant not just for the paperwork but for...everything.

He smiled at her, and she hoped she wasn't kidding herself when she thought she saw understanding in his beautiful blue eyes.

Using her good leg to do most of the work, she actually did manage to step up into the RTA helicopter mostly on her own. Somehow knowing Spence was right there to brace her and keep her from falling made it easier. She looked around the interior for a moment, thinking about the last time she'd been in here, lying across these seats, hurt and bleeding.

Spence climbed in and sat next to her, fussing with the seat belts he'd used then to hold her in place. His mother took the copilot's seat while Ryan settled in and prepared for takeoff. And as the bird came to life, and things started to whir, Abby looked back at them.

"All set?"

"We're good. Let's get out of here."

Abby smiled widely. "Yes, let's. And thank you, Hetty."

Startled, she said, "For what? You're doing everything for me."

"But as long as you're with us, at least we know we'll see a lot more of Spence."

His mother was grinning as she turned back to face front as the sound of the engine increased. Hetty risked a glance at Spence. He was staring out the window as if he hadn't heard a thing.

But he was smiling.

Chapter 22

Ryan and Abby's house was a lovely, almost sprawling place on a rise, with the vaulted roofs and ceilings familiar to Alaska. But the house almost seemed insignificant compared to the view from all sides. Out the back, the mountains towered. From the front, there was a sweeping view all the way down to the sound. Hetty thought she could easily sit in either place for hours and, as it turned out, she sometimes did. In fact she was delighted when, after she'd gotten the okay from the doctor, Abby suggested she do the exercises the therapist had ordered out on the back deck, where she could see the country she would be able to visit again once she was back to a hundred percent.

She'd expected, because she knew what kind of people the Coltons were, that they would see to it she had everything she needed. And she did. The room they'd provided had a queen-sized bed—which she ended up in embarrassingly early, running out of steam shortly after the lovely dinner they'd had—and its own bathroom, and was a very short walk to the huge kitchen. A walk she'd been able to manage alone—with those crutches she both hated and loved—this morning, the day after her arrival. In part inspired by the luscious smell of something baking in the oven.

What she hadn't expected was to find just about every-thing she liked to eat and drink on hand, neatly arranged on the counter and on one shelf in the fridge. They didn't know her that well, did they?

"If you want anything else, just let us know," Abby said from where she was setting up a coffee maker. "Spence did the shopping the day before you were released, but he might have missed something."

Spence had done that? How had he known? Sure, they'd eaten together sometimes, when the length of a job required it, or when it was an RTA gathering, but…had he really been paying that close attention to what she ate? What she ordered at The Cove when the gathering was at the quiet waterfront restaurant? Or what she brought on flights that were going to be long enough she wanted something to snack on?

It seemed impossible, but how else would that specific brand and flavor of crackers be there on the counter? Or, to go with them, that container of her favorite hummus—sold only by that small specialty market—sitting there in the fridge? Even her family didn't know about that partic-ular craving of hers.

So did that mean that, all this time, even amid all the jabbing and poking at each other, he'd still been noticing small things like this? A memory floated up out of her mind and she knew the answer. She thought back to those days in high school, when she'd been assigned to tutor him. The very idea of tutoring a Colton had had her almost wishing she'd never volunteered for the program, for all that she'd been flattered when they'd approached her about it. But the idea that a Colton had needed tutoring had been enough of a surprise that she'd gone ahead.

And one of the first things she'd noticed about the then sixteen-year-old Spence Colton was that he noticed *everything*. He'd been so visually oriented that he seemed to observe and remember everything. And that had eventually been the key, the answer, to his problem with traditional reading.

So why was she surprised now that he had noticed something as simple as what she liked to eat?

"You are all being so kind," she said, feeling awkward enough that it sounded in her voice.

"You," Abby said firmly, "are a crucial part of not just RTA, but the RTA family. And thus our family." She looked over at Hetty as she closed the refrigerator door. "And this was the only way your mother would stay and finish her vacation. Which she needed. You seven have kept her busy for a very long time."

"We have," Hetty said. "But she's been a rock for all seven of us, especially after Dad died. She still is. And if this is what it took for her to get that break she deserves, I thank you all over again."

"I know."

The oven timer dinged and Abby grabbed a potholder and went over to pull out a tin full of wonderful-smelling muffins. She set them to cool then glanced at Hetty, who had taken in a deep breath of the scent, which in turn had made her stomach growl audibly. Abby grinned and tugged one of the muffins out by the paper liner, plopped it on a small plate and slid it over to her, along with the butter dish.

"Butter it now, but I'd give it a minute or two to cool before you stuff it in your mouth."

Abby Colton, Hetty decided then and there, was a delight. She didn't know her as well as she knew her husband, having worked with him for quite a while now, but she should have guessed that a nice guy like Ryan would be married to a nice woman. And luckily for her, she was also someone who baked a wicked-good banana nut muffin. Hetty savored the taste, marveling again at how good food tasted away from the hospital. Alaska might have to import ninety-five percent of its food because of the permafrost, so that even in summer when the surface was green, a few feet down was still frozen, but the Coltons sure brought in the good stuff.

Hetty was used to being on the move most of the day, so it was a bit mentally difficult for her to stay still when her leg started seriously aching. But a perusal of the well-stocked bookshelves she found in Abby's home office made her quickly decide maybe this wouldn't be so bad, after all. She also wasn't used to tiring out in the middle of the day—especially after doing nothing more difficult than getting up now and then from the chair she'd staked out for reading—but they'd warned her it would happen. And so, reluctantly, she'd accepted that an afternoon nap was going to be on the agenda for a few days.

When she woke up after that first nap to a vase full of her favorite flowers, the Alpine Aster, the delicate lavender blossom with the bright yellow center, she felt as if she'd landed in some expensive, full-service hotel.

Having learned the hard way with a near tumble, she moved very slowly to get up, using the crutches she'd this time left next to the bed. The house seemed quiet at the moment, but the door to Abby's office was open, so she peeked in. Spence's mother had been reading something on the screen of a laptop, but immediately looked up.

"Well hello," she said. "How are you feeling?"

"Rested. And better, I think."

"The two go hand in hand, I suppose."

Hetty smiled. "The flowers are lovely. Thank you."

Abby smiled back at her as she got to her feet. "Don't thank me, I only provided the vase. Thank Spence. He stopped by to see how you were doing, and brought those with him. He stopped to gather them on his way here, said they were your favorites."

It was a moment before she could react to that. Spence had been here? In her room, while she'd been asleep? Although, it made no sense that that made her pulse kick up, not after the night they'd spent in the cave. Or maybe it was that those circumstances had been so unique, it didn't count; it was all part of the craziness of that day and night.

"They are my favorites," she said, her throat a little tight.

Was there nothing the man hadn't noticed? She'd bet there were friends she'd had for years who couldn't have come up with everything he had. And to handpick that bouquet...

"This scared us all, Hetty," Abby said quietly. "But especially Spence. I think he had this image of you as indestructible."

Hetty's mouth quirked. "Feeling pretty fragile right now, and I don't like it."

"I'm just glad you're going to be all right, no matter how long the path to get there is."

And that, Hetty decided, was the outlook she needed to adopt. She was going to be all right, eventually. And it very easily could have been worse.

"I might have bled to death, if Spence hadn't been there. If he wasn't always so prepared for anything."

"His father taught him well," Abby said.

"I will never again tease him about lugging that backpack everywhere."

Abby laughed then said, "He's got a run to make today, to one of the fishing camps, but he'll be here for dinner. And he'd better show up because he's supposed to bring dessert from the bakery."

Hetty wondered if he'd hit a home run on that, too, somehow remembering her favorite pecan pie. She decided she wouldn't expect it, but at the same time wouldn't be in the least surprised if he did.

"Now, how about a snack to tide you over until then?"

Abby walked beside her down the hall, matching her slow pace but not making a big deal of it, which Hetty appreciated. She took a seat on one of the high stools at the kitchen counter, grateful, if for no other reason, that they were easier for her to get on and off of since it required less exertion of the very muscles trying to heal. The doctor had told her it would take several weeks for her to be back to her old strength and control, and that, for the first few of those weeks, she'd be seeing a physical therapist here in Shelby.

Belatedly she realized something her joy at getting out of the hospital had pushed to the back of her mind. She wasn't going to be able to drive for a while—at least not her rugged little Jeep, which was a manual transmission that required a functional left leg—but she needed to get to the south end of town three days a week.

"That didn't look like a happy thought," Abby said as she set one of the muffins she'd baked and what looked like a mug of luscious hot chocolate in front of her on the counter.

"I…just realized I can't drive my car for a while," Hetty said. "It's a stick, and I'd never manage the clutch. But I have appointments with the therapist the hospital referred me to in town and—"

"Don't worry, we've got it worked out," Abby said cheerfully. "I'll take you tomorrow, Ryan on Wednesday, and Spence will drive you on Friday and all the next week."

Spence, all week? "Can he afford the time? I know we were booked pretty solid."

"Parker's doing more of the fieldwork for a bit. And he's liking getting out of the office more. And Ryan and Will haven't forgotten much, you know, despite their…semiretirement."

Abby rolled her eyes as she said that last bit, and Hetty couldn't help laughing. "If that's retirement, I'll just keep working, thanks."

"My sentiment exactly," Spence's mother agreed then went back to the subject at hand. "And then, as soon as you're cleared to drive, you can use my car until you're healed enough to get back to the Troll."

Hetty burst out laughing; she'd had no idea anybody outside her family knew her nickname for her army-green, slightly battered Jeep.

But then, she was now realizing just how much a part of the Colton family she already was. Which in turn made

her think of Spence and wonder what, if anything, would
come of those revelations divulged in the shadows of a cave
here in the land of the Midnight Sun.

Chapter 23

"No proof yet," Bobby Reynolds said. "But the new wife says the ex would be more than capable of something like that."

Spence's jaw tightened as he listened to the officer's blunt statement. Reynolds was one of the most senior members of the Shelby Police Department, and while he was a bit stiffly by-the-book, he took any crime that happened in or near his town very seriously. And when it was as serious as this was, he dug in. He might not be the most sympathetic guy around—probably ran out of that years ago, Spence thought—but you could depend on him to find what needed to be found, no matter how long it took.

"They're trying to track her down now," Reynolds said, running a hand over his short, light brown hair, "but she's apparently out of town and no one seems to know where."

"Convenient," Spence muttered with a grimace.

"My thought exactly. They'll keep on it. And if they don't, I will."

"What about the shooter himself?"

"I sent copies of the sketch to all the departments in the area both of your clients and where the ex is—as far as we know—living, to see if anyone recognizes him. In the meantime, everybody here is on the lookout. We'll be talking to anybody who even has the same shoe size, I swear."

Spence knew they'd found some tracks up at the scene because they'd come to look at his hiking boots, to check the sole pattern to eliminate them from the search. They'd also verified his guess on the caliber of the rifle, having found the spent bullet in the tree he'd directed them to. He decided then to go ahead and share his theory, even though it was nothing more than just that, a theory.

"My gut says he's a city guy, but I have no proof of that," Spence said. "Just the way he moved. He made more noise than somebody familiar with the woods and hills would make, so I was thinking he was used to having more noise to cover him, like in a city. Or maybe he wasn't used to a lot of tree branches moving around him."

Reynolds's gaze turned inward, considerately, then he nodded. "It makes sense."

Encouraged, Spence went on. "And he was either trying to miss, is a lousy shot or not used to that rifle. Thankfully."

"More used to handguns in that city of his?" Reynolds asked.

It didn't seem to be a jab, but still Spence said only a cautious, "Maybe. Like I said, no proof, just speculation."

"But the speculation of someone who does know how to move in the backcountry." A slight smile curved Reynolds's mouth, and a glint of amusement showed in his brown eyes. "And someone who's used to carting around people who don't."

"That, too," Spence agreed a bit ruefully.

"I'll keep you posted if anything turns up."

And he would, Spence acknowledged when the man left

to take a call. As he'd thought earlier, Reynolds was nothing if not dependable. And he tended to take anything that disrupted the peace of his little town kind of personally. They were lucky to have the guy.

As he walked back to his car, glad he'd run into Reynolds because it had saved him trying to track him down, he pondered the revelation of that last realization. He'd never thought much about such things like Shelby being lucky to have a cop like him. Or Melissa in the bakery, who, day after day, turned out luscious things like the pecan pies Hetty loved, one of which sat on the passenger seat beside him right now.

Hetty.

That was why he was thinking that way. They'd nearly lost her, so naturally he was thinking that way.

He'd nearly lost her.

He had to suppress the shudder that rippled through him at the thought. He didn't know what would happen next, or where they would go from here, but at least he had hope. That small hope could have been destroyed before it had ever seen the light of day. If their attacker had been a better shot, she could have died out there. That night in the cave would never have happened and he would have spent the rest of his life regretting never having told her the truth, and never knowing that her sniping had been as much a cover as his flirting.

As he headed for his folks' place, a movement above caught his eye. An eagle, not low and searching the water for dinner, but soaring high, in that way Spence had always thought of as flying for the love of it. Kind of like Hetty. He'd never doubted she loved what she did, as much as he loved what he did. Which made them both lucky, he guessed. Loving your work wasn't something everyone had in life.

And now, maybe they would work on something else not everyone had. Another kind of love. The kind he saw every day between his mom and dad, his aunt and uncle. He knew Hetty had seen it, too, in her parents before her father had died. Had she also doubted she would ever find that kind of bond with someone? Could they take whatever they'd started in that cave and build on it?

Damn, you're starting to sound like Lakin, mooning about Troy. When did you become mush?

He knew the answer to his own silent question. He'd turned to mush when he'd found Hetty down and bleeding and thought she was going to die.

He picked up the pace the moment he hit his folks' long driveway up to the house and parked as close as he could get to the front porch. When he got inside, he found his mom and Hetty sitting in the great room, laughing at something. The scene tightened his chest. And when Hetty looked at him with those amazing green eyes, when she saw the pie box he was carrying, with the word *pecan* scrawled on it, she smiled. And no matter how much he tried to tell himself it was because he'd gotten the pie she liked, he couldn't help thinking there was more to it. More to the way she was looking at him, smiling at him.

Maybe even a foundation.

Let the building begin.

If it weren't for the occasional little spike of nerves and the more frequent throb of pain from her leg, Hetty would have enjoyed this evening as much—well, even more, if her little brothers were arguing—as dinner at home with her family. Being able to ask Ryan Colton about the founding of RTA, and how he and his brother had decided to do it in the first place, the stories of how he and Abby had met in San Diego, was fun. They'd skipped the gruesome events that had precipitated the move and gone straight to how much they loved their adopted state.

"Alaska's no place for wusses," Ryan said, and there was pride in his voice, no doubt at how well and how completely his family had adapted.

"She knows that, Dad," Spence said, his gaze fastened on her. "All she has to do is look in a mirror."

"Truer words never spoken," Abby agreed, but Hetty barely heard her. Spence had taken her breath away, not just with those words but with the way he'd looked at her when he'd said them.

In my arms. At last.

The words he'd said that night when they'd been wrapped around each other under the emergency blanket. Courtesy of that huge, ever-present backpack she would never joke about again.

But tonight all she'd been able to manage was to thank him for the lovely flowers. And suddenly she was face to face with the downside of staying here in this lovely house, with people who were taking such good care of her. She couldn't seem to get a moment alone with Spence. He didn't seem particularly concerned about it, and just went on with what probably was, to him, a normal dinner at home with the folks. It was only when she began to doze off on the couch, in spite of the interesting conversation, that he acted.

"Come on," he said, taking her hand and jolting her back to alertness. "You need to get some rest."

Her first instinct, born of years of having to prove herself, was to protest and say she was fine. But she wasn't fine, on a couple of fronts, so she tamped down that reaction and let him help her to her feet. And then startled herself with a sudden wish that he would sweep her up into his arms and carry her, as he had out there in the wild. She even thought about stumbling, intentionally, to see if he would, but that didn't seem fair. Or smart, since his parents were watching and would then think she was weaker than she actually was and hover even more than they already were.

Instead, he handed her the crutches. She grimaced inwardly. But then he said encouragingly, "When your leg's a little stronger, we'll try it with you just leaning on me."

Did he mean that in more than a practical way? Did he mean for her to lean on him in the way a…a girlfriend might?

The moment they were out of sight in the short hallway, she gave into the urge and said, "We need to talk. Don't we?" She hated that she'd ended with that question and in an edgy-sounding tone.

"That can wait until you're stronger, too," he said as he ushered her into the room she was using. Just as she was about to interpret that as avoidance because he'd changed his mind, he leaned in and whispered, "So hurry up, will you?"

And then, to her shock and delight, he backed her up against the wall and kissed her.

Chapter 24

He shouldn't have done it.

Spence stopped just outside the bedroom door he'd closed as he'd left, not ready to face anyone at the moment.

He shouldn't have done it because all his good, responsible resolutions had just been blown to hell. He'd intended to wait until she was well, at least well enough to function on her own. He'd intended to simply be there when she needed him, if only because he knew how stubborn she was about accepting help. He'd intended to be the support she needed right now, nothing else.

He'd never intended to kiss her, especially under his parents' roof, although that modifier made him feel like a rowdy teenager again. But she'd been right there, looking up at him with those eyes. And her lips had parted slightly, as if she'd suddenly needed more air, just as he had. The temptation was overwhelming and he hadn't been able to resist. He simply had to touch, to taste. It wasn't just an urge, it was a necessity.

And then reality had wiped everything out of his mind except for the taste of her lips under his. The feel of her long, taut body against his.

Nice job, Colton. She's just out of the hospital and you're pushing her up against a wall.

It had made the rest of the process of getting her to the bed—and blocking any and all thought about joining her there—awkward and uncomfortable. Not because she'd pushed him away. Oh no. She'd reached up and pulled him closer, as if she'd wanted more. And more. Which had made backing off hard.

Among other things...

Only remembering the doctor's words about getting enough rest and not pushing too much too fast—as if he knew Hetty's nature already—had enabled him to back off. But it hadn't enabled him to do it easily. Or willingly.

Spence gave a sharp shake of his head, gritted his teeth and steeled himself to go face his parents. And stopped dead just inside the great room entry when he realized they were snuggled up on the couch together...kissing.

His first thought was the silly idea that there was something in the air. Something that had not only made his control snap, but theirs.

Vivid memories flashed through his mind of the times when as a kid he'd walked in on them just like this. "Ew, gross!" had been his usual reaction. But now, he felt an odd sort of knot in his gut. After all that had happened, after everything they'd been through, and everything they'd accomplished in spite of it, his parents were still rock-solid, still able to feel like this about each other. And he realized, at the far-too-late age of twenty-eight, how damned lucky he was to have them as an example.

"Hetty all right?" his father interrupted the kissing to ask.

He nodded, hoping they couldn't guess from his unsettled state what had happened right down the hall. He tried to focus on what came next, without relating it to what he'd just done. He had to make a charter drop-off tomorrow, early, as much as he would rather stay close by just in case. But they'd already had to shuffle things around so much, he couldn't mess it up even more by canceling now that Hetty was home safe.

"You're taking her to therapy tomorrow?" he asked his mother, who nodded in turn.

"And I've got her on Wednesday," Dad put in. "After that, she's all yours. We've got your calendar cleared on those days through the end of the second week."

All yours... Did he have to put it like that?

"And if I know Hetty," Mom said, "after that, she'll be stubbornly back to trying to handle everything herself, so you'd better hover."

All he could do was nod. Because, if he spoke, he was afraid he'd give everything away, and he had no right to do that until he and Hetty had had that *talk*. The one he didn't want to have here, where there was every likelihood of an interruption.

"I'll check in when I get back from the drop-off tomorrow," he said as he headed for the front door, thinking that at least he didn't have to worry about Hetty being in good hands. And then, with the door already pulled open, he stopped and looked back at them. "I love you," he said.

Their eyes widened and he took it as proof he didn't say that nearly often enough. The smiles they both gave him made him realize that needed to change. Now.

Nothing like a brush with death to wake a guy up.

The next day, he got back to the RTA office after making what happily turned out to be a routine run to one of their fishing camps further down the sound, and was still filling out the report for Lakin—in that unique but efficient way he had, thanks to a certain high school tutor—when the door opened. He looked up to see his cousin Mitchell stepping in.

"Hey," he said in surprise. As a very successful attorney practicing corporate law, Mitchell—who winced if you shortened it to Mitch—didn't spend much time at RTA, although, like any Colton. he'd be there in an instant if need be. "I thought you were in Anchorage."

"I was. Got back last night, but it was late, so I got some sleep and waited until today."

"How'd it go?" Spence asked, knowing Mitchell had been there giving testimony on a case filed against some bureaucratic agency that had overstepped. It hadn't been his case, but he'd been called as an expert witness.

Mitchell smiled. "The opposition wasn't very happy with me, so I'm taking that as a win."

"Sounds good to me," Spence agreed with a grin.

His cousin lifted a brow at him. "I hear things have been a little crazy around here. How's Hetty?"

"She's going to be fine," he answered firmly. "She's at my folks' place, and Mom's working from home this week to be there with her."

Mitchell smiled. "No wonder I didn't see her at the *Weekly* when I got in this morning." Spence nodded, knowing that his office was right next to the *Shelby Weekly* office. "That sounds like Aunt Abby."

"Yes. It's just like her," Spence agreed, his throat tightening a little all over again at how both his parents had leapt into action when needed.

Mitchell glanced around the RTA headquarters, empty right now, except for Spence. "Kind of kinks things up a bit around here, though, doesn't it, being down a pilot?"

"For a while. But Dad's filling in, and we're using the chopper until the plane's repaired."

Mitchell frowned. "I ran into Officer Reynolds outside my office this morning. He said it had been tampered with?"

Spence nodded, the warmth fading as the barely sublimated anger welled up again. "If anybody less than Hetty had been at the controls, I probably wouldn't be standing here talking to you now."

"But who would ever—"

Spence held up a hand and shook his head. "We don't know for sure yet. Might be somebody connected to a client, or totally unrelated, just some nutjob taking potshots. They're working on it. You know how slow that can go when you're working with little scraps of evidence."

"Too well. Speaking of which, what's this about Hetty finding a dead body up there?"

Quickly, Spence told his cousin what he knew, once again ending with the same exasperation at the lack of progress.

"But your brother is on that one, so I'm betting it'll go faster," Spence said, meaning it.

"It will if Eli has anything to say about it," Mitchell agreed.

"So, what's up for you now?"

The other man grimaced slightly. "I don't know. Things

have been pretty quiet. I've got nothing on the docket at the moment. I mean that thing in Anchorage wasn't even my case."

"So you can go fishing or climb mountains for a while," Spence said. "By yourself, as usual," he added with a wry grin because, just like himself, it was his cousin's habit to trek out solo whenever he had some spare time.

He knew, and he was sure Mitchell did, too, that the family worried about that. Just a little, but some, because… well, Alaska. But to Spence it was worth the risk, to fully experience the vast expanses, to enjoy literally endless summer days and cope with winter nights and single digit temperatures. To savor the pristine white of snow and the crackling ice of the glaciers. And above all else the towering peaks that put what they called mountains in the continental U.S. in a distant second place. He supposed it was the same with his cousin.

"Actually, I'm thinking maybe I should be worried," Mitchell said. "Every time I have a lull like this, something big seems to come along."

"I've had enough of big things for a while," Spence said, his tone dry. "So the next one's yours."

Mitchell gave him an exaggerated side-eye. "Thanks a lot, cuz."

Spence was still laughing as his cousin left. And knew the only reason he had the heart to laugh at all was his family and the fact that Hetty, indeed, was going to be fine.

And it flitted through his mind that he wanted the day to come when he didn't have to separate the two.

Chapter 25

Hetty had been many things in her life, but pampered was not one of them. Her father had been loving but brusque, and had left them far too soon. Which had left her mother too harried with seven children to spend a lot of time coddling each of them. Yet Mom had always been there for her, for all her siblings, caring and caretaking, and Hetty counted herself lucky for that.

But right now she was thinking she could get used to this. Oh, not the rigorous rehab she was going through, although she'd had to take a break just now, after an hour of pushing as hard as she could short of doing new damage. But now, while taking a break out on the back deck, looking up at the mountains whose towering peaks were never clear of snow, making for a beautiful contrast with the summer green of the lower altitudes, she seized on other things to think about so she wasn't so focused on her body's soreness. And life here in the Colton house was quite a change.

It had been three days of both pain and bliss. The rehabilitation part was tough, but if there was anything she needed, anything she wanted, Spence saw that she had it. Sometimes even before she realized she wanted it. To the point where it was making her think about things like mind reading and psychics. One day, it was the cinnamon roll she'd been thinking about. The next, it was that book she'd been wanting to read. And the next, it was the cane she wanted to try as soon as the therapist said she could. That one he'd leaned against the wall right by the door to the bedroom.

"Keep the goal in sight," he'd said simply, and with a casual shrug, as if going out of his way to do this was nothing special. But Spence Colton was definitely something special. Even when she'd been the most irritated at him, she'd never doubted that.

She remembered how in high school she used to watch him with the girls, watch how they all flirted with him, looking at him with what her mother laughingly called "sheep eyes." With his looks, his name and the fact that he'd been the star of both the school's baseball—weather-short season and all—and hockey teams for bait, they'd circled him like hungry fish. She supposed that was how he'd learned to deal with the come-ons so well, because he'd been the target of them from such a young age.

She, on the other hand, had not. Not that there hadn't been interest because as one of the few biracial students on campus she'd been a bit of a novelty, but because she'd had no patience for it and it had showed. That had been why, when she'd been given the tutoring assignment for him, she'd dreaded it.

Suddenly, vividly, a memory shot through her mind, something she hadn't thought of in years. That first day, when Spence had walked into the small study room that was dedicated to the tutoring program. She'd seen him earlier, out near the gym and the baseball diamond, smiling amid a cluster of girls laughing delightedly at something he'd said. But the smile he'd worn then was nowhere to be seen now. And her irritation had broken through the mask of indifference she'd tried to put on.

"Sorry to take you away from your fan club," she had said sharply as he'd entered and dropped a couple of books on the small table.

His head had snapped up and he'd stared at her. And then, in a voice she'd never forget, he had said, "If they knew I was stupid enough to end up here, they wouldn't be interested."

She'd been taken aback, not only by the chill in his tone but the self-disgust, and had truly regretted what she'd said and how she'd said it. Because she knew he wasn't stupid, the director of the program had told her about his math and science and engineering scores, that he was borderline genius in all of those areas. She'd vowed then and there that she would find a way through whatever his problem was, find the method that would work for him.

And she had, she thought now, with no small amount of satisfaction. And it had, as he'd told her with solemn sincerity the day he'd found out he'd passed all his final exams, changed his life. Forever.

She supposed maybe that was the moment. The look in his eyes, the genuineness in his voice when he'd thanked her for saving him, the nothing-less-than-fierce hug he'd given her... She thought maybe that was when she'd fallen. Fallen for the real Spence, the one he kept so well-hidden but that she had seen in every session they'd had.

Of course she'd shoved the feeling aside, because Hetty Amos had had no time for something as silly as high school romance. Or any romance, for that matter. She'd had plans for her future, and even though she'd admired and loved her mother dearly, they hadn't included getting married and having a bunch of kids.

And she had done it. That reaching for planes in the sky she'd done as a child had become her true passion on a school-sponsored small-plane flight to Anchorage for a ceremony for award-winning students. She'd been beyond fascinated not only with the flight but the plane itself, how it worked, and the intricacy of the controls. She'd been so entranced, even the pilots had noticed and had let her sit in the copilot seat part of the way. That was when she'd been certain of her destiny.

Over her mother's fears, as soon as she'd finished high school, she put herself through flight school. Her determination never wavered. It was what she'd been born to do, and she would let nothing stop her. One of her flight instructors, Andrew West, a former military pilot who specialized now in teaching the younger students, seemed to recognize a kindred spirit, and had taken a personal interest. He'd not only taught her, he'd pushed, prodded and demanded her absolute best.

Flying in Alaska is unlike anywhere else in the world. It's not just the mountains, and the fact that dead-end canyons are everywhere, or that you'll be flying at lower altitudes and so have less time in an emergency, or that magnetic variation can be as much as twenty-five degrees, it's also that you're flying over water that's always frigid. Never forget the 1-10-1 rule.

She'd committed that to memory early on. First minute in the water was pure cold shock. After ten minutes, you had muscle failure. And after one hour, you'd be unconscious from hypothermia, and therefore dead. And even if she hadn't memorized it, the test training she'd had to go through would have pounded it home. Nothing like being dumped in that icy water and having to get yourself out of the mockup aircraft and to a pier a hundred yards away to sear it into your brain.

You've got it, Amos. You've got that passion, and you've got the knack, you just need to hone the skills. You need to work harder at it than you've worked at anything, even that fancy top-of-the-class diploma you got.

Hetty smiled at the memory, sighed aloud and went back to work stretching her leg. That, if she set the pain aside, was perhaps the most unsettling aspect of all of this. She was a goer and a doer, and didn't normally spend much time lost in thoughts of the past. But she had twenty-four hours a day now where her brain was free to roam, and even when she was working on the injury, they happened. In the beginning, she had let them, as a distraction from the pain, but now the recollections seemed to be happening all the time.

Except when she was fantasizing about the future. A future she had no guarantee would really happen. Not until she and Spence had that talk they had both hinted at.

So get to work in the now. Start planning instead of remembering. You can fly a freaking airplane, you can figure this out.

Self-directed order given, she began to do exactly that. There had to be a way. Maybe the next time he was here, she could claim cabin fever and ask him to take her outside, somewhere, anywhere. Anywhere away from potential interruptions. Anywhere they could have that discussion. Because she couldn't stand to just loll around here and wonder any longer.

She didn't want to just reclaim the life she'd had, she wanted to start building that new one, the one she'd never really hoped to have until that night in the cave had let her know it might be possible.

You need to work harder at it than you've worked at anything...

Captain West's words came back to her again and, for the first time, she thought they could apply to more than just learning to fly.

Or perhaps it would be a different kind of flying.

Her resolution settled now, she went back to her stretching. She'd done the hardest part of the routine, now it was a matter of keeping the injured tissue and muscles from tightening up too much, keeping the scar tissue to a minimum. She didn't know just how much of a scar she was going to have, but she'd resolved early on that she'd consider it a souvenir, a reminder of that night.

She wondered if there would come a time when she would be telling the story of how it—they—began in a dark, hidden cave, one of those nights that never really became night and—

"You're not pushing too hard, are you, Hetty?"

Abby Colton's voice as she stepped out onto the deck was light, cheerful, and obviously sincere. It had taken Hetty a bit of effort to see the woman as an individual rather than just as Spence's mother and the wife of the founder of RTA, but Hetty felt as if she knew her much better now. And liked her. She'd always read her articles in the local paper, mostly—or so she had told herself—because of her connection to her employer.

But now she was at the point where she could admit it was also because she was Spence's mother.

"I'm through the hard part," she said.

"Good," Abby said as she sat down on the chair closest to where Hetty had stretched out on the mat she did her sessions on. She held out a glass, which Hetty recognized as full of that luscious strawberry lemonade she frequently made.

"Oh, I love this stuff."

Hetty accepted the glass thankfully. She took a long swallow, let out a sigh of satisfaction and appreciation, then licked her lips to be sure she hadn't missed any.

Abby smiled widely. "Now that's the best kind of thank-you."

Hetty took another long drink, then decided what the heck and finished it. Toying with the now-empty glass, she said, "Speaking of thank-yous, I don't know how I'll ever thank you for this," she said, gesturing with her free hand at the house, the deck, the view.

"You're one of the most important components of RTA. It's the least we can do." She grinned. "Besides, I'm under strict orders to see to you today, since Spence is off collecting your baby."

Hetty blinked. All the possible meanings of that phrase shot through her mind and her voice was a little wobbly when she said, "He's what?"

"I know, your precious plane's been sitting up there all this time, but this is really the first chance they've had, with the schedule so messed up."

Oh. The plane. She felt a flush rising to her cheeks and looked away. Abby went on.

"And as Chuck said, it was a bear to get all the parts out here, and it wasn't like anybody could really steal it. But he says he's finally got it flyable, so Ryan flew Spence and his uncle Will out to get her this morning. Then he'll shadow them coming back, just in case."

Hetty knew Will Colton was a fixed-wing pilot, although he hadn't done as much for RTA since they had hired her. But that fact didn't matter to her. What mattered was that it had finally registered exactly where they were going.

"Spence is going back there?" she almost yelped. "To where the shooter was?"

Abby looked puzzled. "To where the plane is. He's the one who knows."

"But what if that guy is still around? What if he's still out there?"

A sudden image of Spence lying on the ground in a pool of blood, dying, shot through her mind and, for a moment, she couldn't breathe. She felt a shudder go through her, tried to stop it, and failed.

"No," she finally blurted. And then all the fears tumbled out in a single rush. "No, he can't go back out there, that guy saw him there that night, too, and he might think Spence saw him, if he's still there he could see him now, and maybe he won't miss this time and—"

She stopped when Abby left her chair and came down beside her on the mat, enveloping her in a rather fierce hug.

"Shh," she soothed. "They're ready for that, Hetty. Armed and ready, I might add. I promise you they are. Ryan and Will would never, ever, let anything happen to

Spence. We've been there before, and if there's a vow we Coltons will never break, it's that one. Nothing happens to our kids."

Hetty gulped in a breath and tried to suppress the shakiness that had gripped her the moment she'd thought of Spence being back where the shooter had tried to kill both of them. It took her a moment or two of clenching her jaw, but she finally got her breathing back to normal.

"Now," Abby said, still in that soothing tone, "would you like to tell me what that was about? Is there something going on between you and Spence I should know about?"

Hetty's gaze shot to her face. She looked away quickly, but was very much afraid she had betrayed herself. "I can't…talk about it."

I can't talk about it until we talk about it. Talk. Talk, talk, talk. When had that become the watchword?

"All right," Abby said. "But may I say one thing?"

Hetty looked back at the kind, caring woman who was Spence's mom. She didn't trust herself to speak, so only nodded.

"I hope it's true. That there's something going on between you. Because you would be the best thing that could happen to him."

With that, she got to her feet, took Hetty's empty glass from her, and went back into the house. Leaving Hetty staring after her, her eyes stinging a little at the pure honesty and hope that had been in those words.

Chapter 26

His father hadn't had time to look around up here before, when the focus had been on getting Hetty to the trauma center. And then, after that, it had been a crime scene. Actually, two crime scenes that overlapped. And with his son involved in one, and his nephew investigating the other, Spence should have guessed Dad would want to look around now. Neither his father nor his uncle would ever take a threat to one of their offspring lightly. Not with the family history being what it was.

Once Spence had pointed out where the areas involved were, he'd left them to it. He was happy just doing what he could to clean up the cockpit of the plane. Chuck had gotten the fuel pump fixed so that it wouldn't be an issue during takeoff, which was the main time the high-wing aircraft needed it, but there was still a bit of debris from the window that had been shot through, and he didn't really want to chance sitting on broken glass.

And then there were the markings the forensics people had made, showing where they'd found evidence for the photographs they'd taken. He didn't want those there when Hetty was able to get back to the pilot's seat.

He'd thought about trekking up the hill with them, to

where the body had been buried, but decided there was no reason. If he knew his cousin Eli, they'd combed that area so thoroughly they'd probably scared away any scavengers for weeks. And there was no way seeing the spot now would erase the image in his mind of the half-buried body. Besides, he'd had no real desire to revisit the grim site anyway.

The cave, now...

The moment the idea hit, he was seized with a sudden need that seemed undeniable. He climbed out of the plane and jumped down to the beach. He headed up the hill, not quite sure where this urgency had come from. He made it there a lot faster than he had that night, although the memories were so vivid they made him feel just as wound up as if it were that night again, and Hetty was in his arms and bleeding.

He barely slowed for the steeper parts of the climb, and managed not to even look over toward the little waterfall where it had happened.

You think you're rattled? She found the body and then got shot, she's the one who should have been a basket case. But no, not Hetty. She held it together, because that's what she does.

He stepped behind the big Sitka spruce and sidled through the narrow cave entrance. He had to stop for a moment to let his eyes adjust to the dim light. It didn't look like anyone—or anything—had been in there. He supposed whatever scent they'd left behind had kept the wary wild creatures clear. Stupid, vicious humans, however, were another matter, so he trod carefully.

Once he was certain the cave was empty, he walked over to the little alcove where they had spent that long, emotion-filled night. He hadn't really intended to do this, so he only had the flashlight from his phone to use to scan the area. He found some paper wrappings from the gauze, which he automatically picked up and stuffed in his pocket. His instinct about keeping the wilds free of unnatural litter was strong.

His stomach clenched when he found some bloodied cloth lying where Hetty had been. He'd forgotten he'd pulled one of his spare shirts out of the pack and used it to try to staunch the bleeding. The dread he'd felt then washed through him again now.

The next thing he knew, he was crouched down near the cave floor, feeling as if his legs had suddenly given out. The light from the phone lit up a dark spot on the floor of the cave. He knew it was blood, Hetty's blood, and nausea churned his gut. He should have known then how badly hurt she'd been. He should have tried to get her out of there and on the way to help right then, shouldn't have tried to wait until morning even though she had insisted she'd be fine. He should have—

"Spence!"

Even coming through the speaker of the RTA walkie-talkie clipped to his belt, his father's voice sounded…sharp. Harsh. Angry?

At his next thought, dread suddenly swamped him all over again. Had that not been anger he'd heard in Dad's voice, but fear? He hadn't heard any unusual noise, certainly not a shot, but…

He spun on his heel and ran to the mouth of the cave. Froze there, listening. Automatically, his hand slipped down to his belt, checking his knife.

"Spence Colton, get your sorry butt back here right now!"

He heard them both now: anger and fear. But if Dad was calling him back, the threat wasn't there, or wasn't active. Or anywhere near…or he wouldn't be shouting. So he scrambled out of the cave and down the hill, trying to focus on getting there rather than what he might find when he did.

The moment he cleared the tree line, he saw Dad and Uncle Will standing near the helicopter. Had it been tampered with? Was the crazy guy still around? He started to run, and both men turned then, obviously spotting him. For an instant, he thought they both almost sagged a little, as if they'd each let out a huge breath. Of relief?

His brow still furrowed, he slowed when he got closer. He stopped a few feet away, warily. Because both his father and his uncle were not only holding their rifles, they looked…furious.

"What the hell were you thinking?" His father rarely yelled, and even more rarely swore, but he was doing both now. "Taking off like that and not letting us know?"

"I just went back to the cave because—"

"I don't care where, or why, damn it. You were out of sight without a word, when we're within a few yards of where some nutjob tried to kill you!"

Belatedly—far too belatedly—realization hit. His father had been scared, all right. But not for himself. For him.

It all tumbled into place; another time when a Colton had been found too late. The aunt he'd never known, who had been his father's little sister. And for the first time Spence thought of that family history in today's terms, of how he would feel if something had happened to Kansas. He would carry the scar forever and it would influence his reactions for the same length of time. He realized that now because he already knew he would carry the memory of his panic over Hetty the same way, for that same forever.

"I'm sorry, Dad," he said humbly. "I didn't think." He glanced at his uncle. "You, too, Uncle Will. It was stupid. I should have at least used the radio to check in first."

The two men looked a little surprised. And a bit deflated, which he hoped meant he'd taken a bit of the anger out of them. Not that they didn't have the right to be, but he hated the feeling and wanted it gone.

Uncle Will, ever a wise man, nodded in acceptance then excused himself from the scene to go down to the plane, leaving them alone. And when his father spoke again, it was calmer, although a bit of an edge remained.

"Why did you go back to the cave?"

"I…wanted to clean up," he said, gesturing with the shirt he was still holding. His father's gaze locked on the blood-stained garment and he winced. "We left kind of a mess, in all the rush to…to…"

"Save Hetty's life?" Ryan Colton suggested softly.

Spence met his father's steady gaze, swallowed tightly and blinked a couple of times before giving up on speech and simply nodding.

"I get the idea something else happened up there that night that made you want to go back there."

Not ready for this, not until he knew for sure where he and Hetty stood, he muttered, "Just wanted to be sure we hadn't lost anything up there."

"I think," Dad said slowly, "that you didn't lose any-thing. But just maybe you found something."

Dad had always been too smart to fool for long.

Chapter 27

Hetty was glad when Spence left her alone at the therapy clinic. Not that she wanted him gone, she would much rather have been someplace quiet and private with him now that they were finally away from his parents' house. But she was still new at this therapy thing, and she didn't want him seeing her whimper when the therapist pushed her.

The fact that she had asked the woman to push her as hard as she could without doing damage—she wanted to be back on her feet, sans crutches or even the cane, as soon as possible—didn't mean it didn't hurt like crazy or that she didn't yelp now and then.

And so she'd asked Spence not to hang around and watch, and Mrs. Cowell, who dealt with him like the former marine she was, convinced him of the wisdom of finding something else to do for a couple of hours.

This was not, Hetty thought as she gritted her teeth to do another leg raise, like it was portrayed in the movies. And the next time she saw a film where the protagonist got shot in the leg and the next day was up walking around with barely a limp, she was going to boo and hiss audibly. Maybe throw something at the screen if she was at home.

She pushed harder, until she could feel the tears gathering in her eyes from the pain. Her gut wanted her to push on through, but the therapist had cautioned her the first day that that could be one of the worst things to do.

"You need to listen to your body," she had said warningly. "A little pain is fine, and expected. Agony, not so much. It will set you back, give your body more healing to do, and this will take even longer."

With that echoing in her mind, Hetty eased up until it only hurt, not felt like her leg was tearing apart.

"I have to say," Mrs. Cowell said when she finally called a halt and led her to one of the tables where she would do some massage and heat therapy to promote further healing, "you're the most determined patient I've had in a long time. You're doing well, Hetty."

"Enough for you to give me an estimate on when I'll be back to normal, Mrs. Cowell?"

"I think you'd better call me Liz. We're going to be seeing a lot of each other. But in answer, I'd say a year or so," the older woman said as she worked with nimble hands on Hetty's leg. "That's assuming there's no permanent nerve damage too great to ignore."

Hetty felt a chill ripple over her. She focused on the time span rather than the maybe in the statement, because right now that's what scared her most.

"A year?"

With a tiny quirk of her mouth that told Hetty she was about to get one of those comparisons she loved to make, the therapist said, "I assumed you meant back to where you were before this happened. I'd say you'll be back to functional much sooner, if you keep working this hard. Another week like this, and maybe you can try that cane your man came in and got for you."

Hetty let out a breath of relief. But then the last of the woman's words truly registered. "Wait, who got the cane?"

Liz's brow wrinkled. "The guy we just chased out of here? Spence Colton?"

Hetty felt a flood of warmth inside her. She knew that Spence had brought the cane into her room for inspiration—which she'd needed after the worst parts of these sessions—but she hadn't realized he'd been the one to actually come here and get it.

They were wrapping up before Liz spoke about Spence again. "He's a good man," she said, her tone devoid of any of her usual prodding or teasing. "I'd hang on to that one if I were you."

"We're...still working that out."

The therapist smiled widely. "Judging by the way he looks at you, it's already worked out in his mind."

Hetty's gaze shot to her face. She'd already realized the therapist noticed everything and sensed even more, so she risked the question. "You really think so?"

The tough, relentless woman's expression softened in a way Hetty had not seen before. "He looks at you the way my Matt used to look at me."

Used to? Hetty glanced at the woman's left hand, where a simple gold band adorned her ring finger, then back at her face. The truth was there in her eyes, in the aching sadness, before she confirmed it with words.

"I lost him a few years ago. He was KIA overseas," the woman said quietly.

Hetty couldn't stop herself, she reached out and clasped

that hand, her palm over that ring. She didn't want to say the usual, trite platitudes, which had always seemed useless to her. So instead she said, just as quietly, "He chose well."

The woman's eyes brightened and she knew somehow she'd found the right words. "We were good together."

There was a sound from the doorway and they both looked. It was Spence, who apparently had just made the other therapist—a young man about a foot shorter than he was—laugh. Liz looked back at Hetty.

"Don't waste time you can never get back," she said softly, and there was an amazing combination of remembered pain and goodwill in her voice and her expression.

"You're right," Hetty said decisively. "That ends today."

Back on the crutches—which she was now determined to be rid of after that two weeks Liz had mentioned—she made her way toward the door. Spence was still just outside the door, now looking at something on his phone. She didn't think she'd made any noise, but his head came up sharply and he turned to look as if he'd somehow sensed her coming.

And she thought she'd go through any amount of this hell to see the smile that spread across his face when he saw her.

He looks at you the way my Matt used to look at me...

She was done wasting time.

"Do you have a run this afternoon?" she asked him without preamble.

"No," he said, sounding startled. "I cleared the day. I've got nothing until tomorrow."

"Good. We're going to have that talk."

He drew back slightly, either startled again or...wary. Well, if it was wary, she wanted to know now. Before she let herself fall any further than she already had. Maybe he'd decided that night in the cave had been a mistake, or a hallucination, or maybe he'd only been trying to placate her because she'd been hurt. She didn't know, but it was past time she found out. It wasn't like her to be this indecisive, to have let this drift along for nearly two weeks. But she wanted this so much, maybe she was just afraid of the answers she'd get.

So when did you become a coward?

She wasn't, she told herself firmly. The dodging ended now.

"Where are we going?" Spence asked after they were back in his SUV, still sounding somewhat nervous.

"Somewhere where we can look at this place we love," she said.

Yet again, he looked surprised, but she saw one corner of his mouth twitch, as if he liked what she'd said. She'd meant it, she did love this place, although maybe not quite in the "get out there and learn every inch of it from the ground up" way he did. No, she preferred flying over it, where she could see the incredible vastness, the amazing range, from the water of the sound to the towering mountains, with every variation in between.

She especially savored this time of year, despite the lack of an actual nighttime. She loved the way the snow forever on the peaks contrasted with the fresh green of new growth below and, in turn, with the deep blue of the water. It made her heart swell; made her feel lucky that this was where she'd been born and raised.

"I got a text from Officer Reynolds," he said as they

stopped at one of Shelby's few traffic signals. "He said Portland may have a line on the ex-wife, and he'll let us know."

"If it turns out to be her, remind me never to set foot in Portland again," she said as the light changed.

A few minutes later, when Spence pulled the SUV to a stop atop a slight rise just outside of town, where they could sit and look at everything she'd just thought about, she wondered not for the first time if the man could read her mind.

Her stomach gurgled a little but she ignored it. Food could wait. This could not. And then Spence reached into the back seat and came up with a small cooler. He opened it, dipped in, and showed her a bundle wrapped in paper. She knew at her fist whiff that it was one of the delicious roast beef sandwiches from the shop just above the marina.

"They said it was your favorite," Spence said.

"It is," she agreed, impressed yet again, both that he'd thought of this at all, and especially that he'd bothered to find out what she particularly liked. And in view of that, she decided eating could come first. But she'd do it fast.

"Then let's go sit down out there and eat. You're burning up a lot of energy in that therapy," he said. "Mrs. Cowell is quite a taskmaster."

"She said I should call her Liz. I feel like I've been honored."

"I can see why."

"We're pushing for me to be off the crutches after two weeks." She gave him a sideways look. "And on to using the cane you got for me."

He didn't even react. As if it were the most obviously normal thing in the world for him to go out of his way to both pick up the device and think to place it where it would inspire her to work toward it.

Judging by the way he looks at you, it's already worked out in his mind.

She hoped the taskmaster was right.

Chapter 28

Spence was really glad he'd stopped and picked up lunch. He knew it was just a delaying tactic. But so what? Was any guy ever not nervous about "the talk"?

He got out of the SUV and grabbed the tarp he always carried in the back, because you never knew up here when you might need to protect something from an unexpected burst of rain or snow. He walked over to the spot he frequented himself, with the best, most glorious view down to the marina, over the sound and to the mountains on the other side.

He busied himself a little more than necessary before going back to get Hetty. And lectured himself while he did it. Either she had meant what she'd said in the cave, or she hadn't. Hetty was inherently honest, but maybe she'd been too rattled or hurting too much to dig deep. Or maybe she had been thinking she needed him to get out of there, so she'd better not make him mad.

No. That wasn't Hetty. She would never admit to what she had that night if it wasn't true, even if she was in pain.

Would she?

When he'd helped her over to the chosen spot and they'd settled in, she took the sandwich while he reached into

the small cooler, brought out and popped open two cans
of soda.

He chewed his own first bite of roast beef sandwich a
bit more thoroughly than was really necessary. What did
he know about it? He'd never in his life been serious about
a woman before. At least, not as serious as he was now.

Maybe because you were waiting for her.

He stopped chewing. Sat there staring out over the vista
that felt like a part of him down to his soul, with a mouth-
ful of meat, cheese and the tangy sauce that gave it the
kick he liked.

Could it be true? Could that be another reason, maybe
the real reason, he reacted the way he did when clients
would come on to him? He'd never really considered it before, but after that night in the cave, he'd thought about it a
lot. He had realized that it was like flipping a switch; that
he'd be going along just fine until some woman started the
game and, almost with an audible click, he'd turn on that
Spence, the one who could banter like the biggest play-
boy in town. And all the time, underneath, he'd known
he was anything but. That it was the mask he put on. The
protection.

But he'd never really wondered if there was another reason he did it, why he made certain to keep those interactions
on the surface, essentially meaningless. Never wondered if
there was a reason he'd never been even slightly tempted to
hang on to one of those freely given phone numbers after
the client—and some of them had been pretty darned attractive—was on the way back to wherever she'd come from.

But now he wondered if it was that, somewhere down

deep, he'd known it would never turn into anything because that part of him was already taken.

By Hetty Amos.

He finally swallowed that very well-chewed bite. Stared down at the sound below, at the sunlight dancing on the water, at the cargo ship heading out after unloading whatever portion of its load had been sent to Shelby. He knew in some places they were considered unsightly, but in Shelby they were welcomed, bringing in things from far away. Of course, pretty much everything was far away from Shelby, so if something you wanted or needed was out of stock, you waited. And waited. His gaze shifted to the ever-snowcapped mountaintops, and once again deemed it well worth it.

"It's wonderful to love where you live, isn't it."

Hetty said it as if it were a given, not a question. And suddenly he realized this was the key, this was the way to say what he wanted to say, because he knew she would understand.

"Yes. And I especially love the hidden places I've never told anyone about, places where I never take anyone."

She drew back slightly, her head tilting as she studied him. Hetty-like, instead of asking what places, she asked simply, "Why?"

He sucked in a deep breath and took the plunge. "Because they're special to me, and I wouldn't want to show them to anyone who wouldn't love them as I do. There's a spot up on the ridge—" he gestured up and to the east "—where you can see three of the lakes, the sound, and on a clear day all the way to Mount St. Elias. There's a place in Wrangell where I've been watching a family of Canadian lynx grow up and coexist with a herd of Dall sheep. And a spot lower down where I actually collided with a flying squirrel. Or vice versa."

She was staring at him now, and he knew she hadn't missed the significance of this outpouring, right after he'd said he never told anyone about these special places. But he said what he needed to say anyway.

"I want to show you all of those, Hetty. And so many more. Places so beautiful you have to remind yourself to breathe. So amazing, you're thinking it has to be special effects. Places I've hoarded, kept to myself, because there wasn't anyone who'd look at them or from them and feel what I feel."

"I would," she said softly.

"I know. That's why you need to get well fast, so I can show them to you. All of them."

"Spence."

It was all she said, and he didn't quite know how to interpret it. A spark of fear careened through his brain, that he'd misinterpreted everything. It wouldn't be the first time. But he had to know, and he had to know now. And so it came out a little bluntly.

"I meant what I said that night in the cave. Did you?"

He thought he saw her take in a breath. Then she looked up, holding his gaze steadily. And said, softly, almost reverently, "Every word."

His heart seemed to miss a beat then race to catch up. "All this time…" he said and stopped because he had no idea how to finish. But Hetty finished it for him.

"We've been hiding, me behind sarcasm, you behind flirting. We've wasted a lot of time."

"We have. That stops now."

"Agreed."

A vista as vast as the one they were looking at in reality seemed to roll out in his mind. A future, built on a foundation started more than a decade ago, starring the woman who had changed his life then and would change it again now.

He reached out and with his thumb gently wiped away the trace of that tangy sandwich sauce from the corner of her mouth. That mouth… He wished he had leaned in and kissed it away. Her lips parted, and her tongue crept out as if to taste that spot he'd touched. It was too much and his resistance—resistance that was merely habit, now that they'd admitted out here in the brilliant light of day as opposed to under that Midnight Sun—vanished.

He slipped a hand around the back of her neck in the same moment she reached up to cup his cheek, sending a ripple of luscious sensation through him. And then his mouth was on hers and the ripple became a wave. He let her lead, because it seemed the thing to do. And she did, tasting, probing, until his control snapped. The next thing he knew they were sprawled on the canvas he'd laid out, arms around each other, deep into a kiss he never wanted to end.

It was everything he'd ever thought it would be in those rare times when the idea crept around his defenses and into his imagination. No, it was more. It was incredible. Staggering. Maybe even astonishing.

What it wasn't was impossible. Not anymore.

After all these years, after all the sniping and mocking, and his own fakery and pretending, this was what was real. This was what they'd been hiding.

This was what he'd always wanted but been afraid to go after.

And when they finally broke the kiss, they simply stared at each other, blue eyes boring into green, and Spence knew he had never in his life felt anything more right than that kiss and Hetty in his arms.

He wondered if the smile that he couldn't stop looked half as goofy, as giddy, as he felt. And if Hetty's smile in return was at how silly he must look or because…she felt the same way. He didn't have to wonder long.

"That," she said softly, "was almost worth the wasted time."

An emotion he'd only ever felt when looking at one of those special, secret places he was going to take her to welled up inside him. The only word he could think of for it was beyond corny, but it was the only word that fit.

Joy.

"I guess we really needed our cage rattled to get out of our old rut."

"Well, that's one of the better mixed metaphors I've heard lately," Hetty said, and he knew she was using that old, familiar, tutoring tone of voice on purpose.

Spence laughed and the elation he was feeling practically echoed in the sound of it. He wanted to seize this moment and hang on to it forever.

Just as he wanted to do with Hetty.

Images of the life they could build, here in this place they both loved, unrolled in his head like some video stream. She could move out of her tiny apartment, maybe into his place. Or if she didn't want that, they'd find a new place for both of them. Some place private, where they could pursue this electric connection they had.

He wasn't foolish enough to think there wouldn't have to be some give and take, some adjustments on each side, but they'd do it. They'd do it because it was meant to be, they'd just been fighting it for years. They would—

A loud cough from rather close by made them both jump. They jerked around to see Officer Reynolds standing there.

"Sorry to bother you," he said, "but I saw your SUV up here, Spence, and had some news you need to hear."

Spence went very still. He heard Hetty suck in a breath. They both started to get up, but Reynolds crouched down until he was at eye level with them. His normally neutral, sometimes-thoughtful expression had been taken over by a furrowed forehead and concerned eyes. Bobby Reynolds took his job very seriously, and Spence again had the thought that he hadn't appreciated the small-town cop nearly enough.

"We heard from the PD in Portland, finally. They're really strapped right now, so it took them a while, but…they found your client's ex."

The man hesitated and Spence braced himself, already guessing what was coming next from his somber demeanor.

"Get it said," he told him, reaching out to grip Hetty's hand in his, squeezing it gently.

Reynolds nodded. "All right. They kept on her, and she finally admitted it. She hired somebody to follow her ex and his new wife up here and kill them both."

Chapter 29

Spence heard Hetty's smothered gasp at Reynolds's words, but he wasn't surprised at all. He'd been expecting this ever since he'd heard about the ex-wife. Still, his voice was tight when he spoke again.

"Hired...who?"

He knew the answer to that, too, before Reynolds spoke. "We don't know. All we have is the name Strauss, and it's probably an alias." The cop grimaced. "Barton told me that was the cover name of one of the most prolific hitman ever known, who committed from a hundred to five hundred hits for Murder, Inc., back in the thirties."

"History student or delusions of grandeur?" Spence asked, his tone sour.

"Who knows," Reynolds answered. "I'd lean toward delusions, given his inefficiency."

"For which I'll be eternally thankful," Hetty said fervently, the first thing she had said since this had started.

As will I. Again the image of her down and bleeding tried to take over Spence's mind, but he made himself focus on the subject at hand. "The Creedmoor round isn't going to help much if you don't find the weapon, right?"

Barton nodded. "It's efficient and cheap, so it's all over."

"Low recoil," Spence said, remembering his thoughts about the shooter being maybe a city guy. "Maybe the he's not used to rifles. Or more used to up-close-and-personal weapons."

"Could well be," Reynolds agreed. "They're working on it down in Portland, and we're doing what we can from here. The ex said she found him online, through a connection she wouldn't give up. We don't know how she found out RTA was who they'd booked the trip with, but apparently she did."

"So he knew right where to look," Hetty said.

Reynolds nodded. "Yes. And he told her he'd been to Alaska once before."

Spence couldn't help snorting. "Like that makes him an expert."

He hated people like that. People who thought they knew it all when they knew nothing. It made him recall how neighboring Valdez had begun as a landing port for miners during the gold rush in 1897, and how they'd been conned into thinking something called the Valdez Glacier Trail existed and would lead them directly to the rich, untouched gold fields. That it had turned out to be a hoax promoted by steamship companies to sell tickets, a hoax that had cost many lives and was a sore spot with any local who knew the history.

"I get the feeling that if he was as good as he told her he was, we wouldn't be here talking now," Reynolds said.

Meaning one or both of them would be dead. "Then I'm glad he wasn't," Hetty said heatedly. "This was bad enough."

Reynolds looked at her as if to go on, but hesitated.

"She can take it," Spence said.

That got him a flashing smile from Hetty. But the smile died when Reynolds said, "He knows that you saw him."

Spence had figured that out early on, because there'd been no other reason for the shooter to go after them so strongly once he'd discovered his true targets had not kept their part of his evil bargain.

"He knows Hetty did. I think I was just insurance."

Reynolds nodded. "Maybe, but I kind of doubt he'd risk that you didn't see him. A hired gun isn't usually the type to leave loose ends."

Spence's brow creased. "But he's not from here. Maybe he'd just head back to wherever home is and figure we're far enough away we'd never find him."

"Could be." Reynolds's mouth twisted wryly. "Lots of people from down there think we're a different country anyway. So maybe he's gone and will never come back. But do you want to pin your lives on a maybe?"

"But he doesn't know who we are," Hetty said. "I mean other than we're from RTA."

Reynolds grimaced. "You're all over the RTA website. Named and labeled as locals. In a town of less than four thousand, that narrows his search a lot already. And it's clear that you're the one who flies the floatplane, and Spence is the premier guide in the area, if not the entire state. And in case you haven't looked lately, there are a ton of photos of the two of you with various guests. It's easy to extrapolate that you're usually together."

Spence knew that, in light of the subject matter, it was silly to feel a pleasant little jolt at those last three words, but he couldn't seem to help it.

...you're usually together.

He wanted that to be the mantra for the rest of their lives. He wanted it to be just as true fifty years from now as it was today. He wanted them to be like his parents were, still in love after all these years and all they'd been through.

And he'd do whatever it took to make that happen.

The first thing he had to do was keep Hetty safe, because Reynolds was right, they were all over the website, with pictures clear enough to make them recognizable to anyone who took the time to look. And while the hired gun might not be the best shot—at least, not out here in the backcountry—they couldn't assume he hadn't done his homework.

"The state troopers are being good about sharing information, and I'll pass along anything that's relevant," Reynolds said. "But until we nail this guy down, watch your back."

When Reynolds left them, with assurances they were doing all they could, Spence sat for a moment longer before he could bring himself to meet Hetty's eyes. The incident at the camp was one thing, knowing a hired killer was afraid you'd seen and could identify him was something else altogether.

When he finally shifted his gaze, he saw that she looked troubled but not panicked. But then, Hetty never panicked. She was a lot more likely to get angry about a threat than scared.

He mentally abandoned his wishful thinking about her moving into his place with him. She was better off at the big house, with more people around to keep an eye out. In fact, he'd best stop by his place, grab some things and stay there himself until this was resolved. Better to have three people there looking out for her. He needed to tell his folks about this anyway, so they could be on guard.

So much for that grand seduction scene I was imagining.

"What was that face for?" Hetty asked.

"You don't want to know," he muttered. "Come on, let's go. I need to tell Mom and Dad about this."

She didn't resist. In fact, she nodded quickly when he mentioned his folks. But once he'd gotten up and helped her—which she did try to refuse, but relented when he mentioned that speed was kind of important at the moment—to her feet, she slanted him a troubled look.

"Maybe I shouldn't stay there," she said. "It might put them in danger, too."

"The more eyes watching out, the better," he said shortly as he folded up the tarp they'd been sitting on. "I'll stay there, too. And I have to let Kansas and Parker know about this, too."

"But if I went somewhere else, they wouldn't need to worry."

"Fine," he said shortly, finishing with the tarp and looking at her. "You can move into my place and I'll cancel all my upcoming jobs—"

"You can't do that!"

"I can if you're going to let this clown decide what you do. Which," he added when she glared at him, "is totally unlike you, so I'm going to assume you're just worried about everybody else instead of yourself."

Her expression changed completely. The distress faded away, to be replaced by something else, something warmer, gentler, something almost...pleased? As if he'd somehow, despite the worry that wanted to swamp him, managed to find the right thing to say to her.

"What?" he finally asked when she continued to just look at him.

"You really do know me," she said softly.

All traces of anger faded away, as if she had the power to erase them with those simple words. Or the way she said them. Or the way she looked at him when she did. He didn't know. And right now he didn't care.

"That's because I love you."

He said it, knowing this could easily be the worst possible time, knowing this wasn't at all the kind of romantic setting he would have preferred, knowing he'd intended to play it safe and wait until she said it first. But none of that mattered now. It was the truth, and he'd had to say it now in case things went bad and he didn't get the chance later.

She was staring at him, looking a little shocked. She couldn't be surprised, could she? Or was her reaction because he'd actually said the words? He didn't know. The only thing he knew for sure was that he didn't want her to say the words back at him—not now, not as a reflex kind of reaction. He wanted them from her in the same way he'd given them—because he hadn't been able to stop them.

"Let's go," he said abruptly, bending to pick up her crutches and hand them to her. He tucked the folded tarp under his left arm, then grabbed up the cooler and shifted it to his left hand so his right was free to help her if she needed it. The ground was uneven up here, and better safe than sorry.

She took the crutches and began to make her way back to the vehicle. She didn't say another word.

But she was smiling.

Chapter 30

Because I love you.

The words Hetty had never, ever, expected to hear played on a seemingly endless loop in her head. And all the while as she made her way rather laboriously back to the car, she was aware that Spence was right there. Not forcing his help on her, but right there just in case.

A bit of rueful self-understanding went through her mind. Nobody knew better than Spence how irritated she got when people insisted she needed help she didn't need. She'd certainly snapped at him more than once for his assumptions she couldn't handle something herself. But after how attentive he'd been since she'd been hurt, how—*face it, girl*—how sweet he'd been, she realized it was just who he was underneath the carefree exterior she now knew was a shield of sorts between himself and those who might judge him for that brain quirk he'd been born with.

Despite the effort with the crutches on this uneven ground, she kept smiling. She couldn't seem to help it.

Because I love you.

Why wouldn't she be smiling, after that?

She was a little puzzled by his demeanor after the words had come out. He'd seemed to be…she wasn't sure what to call it. She was only sure that, unlike most people would be, he wasn't waiting to hear her say the words back to him. In fact, he'd acted almost as if he didn't want her to say it. As if what he'd said didn't change…well, everything.

Hetty gave herself a mental shake. She needed to remember the news Officer Reynolds had just dropped on them; that not only had that man been a hired killer, he could now be after them. She wanted desperately to believe he truly had gone back to where he'd come from, never to darken Alaska's door again, but as Reynolds had said, Did they want to risk their lives on a maybe?

Spence was so quiet on the drive back toward his folks' house she couldn't help wondering if he was regretting what he'd blurted out. Was that why he hadn't pushed her to say it back to him? Had it come out of some emotion, some weak spot in his armor that he now regretted?

"Are you okay for a bit longer?" he suddenly asked. "I need to stop by the office."

"Fine," she said. "I'd like to see Lakin, if she's there."

"She'll be there. Place would fall apart without her."

She hesitated then said, "I'm going back to your parents' place. You're not really going to cancel all your upcoming jobs, are you?"

He gave her a sideways glance. "No. I can't really. Parker's covering, but he can only do so much alone."

"I know." She sighed. "Even your dad and uncle are having to come back to work."

She heard him chuckle and looked up, startled. "How's it feel to know it takes two grown men to replace you?"

She couldn't help it, she burst out laughing. "Hey, and you," she said. "You've been too busy taking care of me."

He shifted his gaze back to the road as they neared the turn to RTA. "Mutually exclusive," he said.

"What?"

"I can't be too busy if I'm taking care of you." His voice sounded a little gruff, as if he were trying to be his usual smart-mouthed self and failing.

Hetty felt a stinging in her eyes and blinked rapidly to hold back the welling tears. She swallowed past the tightness in her throat, thinking oddly that while she'd been brought to tears by pain a couple of times in therapy, the difference was unmistakable.

When they arrived, Spence was right behind her as she maneuvered up the three steps to the entrance to RTA. Not beside her, as he'd been before, but behind her, no doubt figuring if she fell, it would be backward. But he didn't, as he once had, offer to just lift her up, nor did he take her arm to steady her; he let her make the short ascent herself.

"Liz said I wasn't helping you by...well, helping you all the time," he said when they were on the porch, as if he felt an explanation was required.

"I know. I have to do as much as I can by myself, even if having to go so slow drives me nuts."

He did open the door for her and hold it, but she quickly decided that wrestling with a big, heavy, wooden door while hanging on to her crutches and keeping her balance was a three-way battle she wasn't quite ready for. Besides, he'd do that for anyone. He was just...polite. She'd seen him do it recently, when he'd held the door to Roaster's open for Mr. Harper from the hardware store, who'd had his hands full. That had been—was it really only two weeks ago today, on the Fourth of July? It seemed like it should be much longer ago, so much had happened since.

And he was kind. Like when he'd comforted that little boy whose dog had been lost, and in fact had found the critter a couple of blocks away.

And thoughtful, as he'd proved when all her favorite foods had showed up in his mother's kitchen.

And she had been too wrapped up in sniping at him for flirting with clients to notice. Too busy doing that to realize that it was all a cover. A protective front. She had the feeling she'd underestimated the amount of mockery and teasing he'd likely undergone in school before they'd had that breakthrough.

She'd always thought he hadn't wanted to go to college because he'd already known his future was with RTA. But maybe part of it had also been that he'd had enough school to choke on. And she couldn't really blame him. After all, she'd chosen her own path, too, forgoing college for flight training.

The thought made her smile. Maybe they were more alike than she had ever realized. She'd had her own kind of protections in place in school. She'd always known she got second glances because of her mixed heritage. More even than Lakin because, as an Inuit, her ancestors were at least native to the area. But Hetty's grandfather had been the first of her family born here, a few years before Alaska had become a state in 1959, and the fact that she was a third-generation Alaskan had always been her armor against anyone who made unwise comments. Honest questions were fine, it was the smart-mouths she took off at the knees.

Spence had just closed the door behind them when Lakin came out of the back office into the lobby area. She spotted them immediately.

"Hetty!"

Lakin ran toward them with her arms extended, as if she were going to throw them around her. Hetty saw the moment when she realized that might not be a good idea—Had that been Spence making that low "ahem" kind of sound?—and she slowed down. When she was close enough, Lakin reached out and gave her a gentle hug, quite a difference from the high-speed collision it could have been. Which could have been disastrous for Hetty.

"It's so good to see you here," Lakin exclaimed. "We've all been so worried, and we've missed you so much."

Hetty smiled widely. She'd missed the long talks she and Lakin always had. And she sent out a mental jab to her brother to quit taking this wonderful person for granted and put a little—no, a lot—more effort into the relationship. Because she wanted this sister of the heart to become one for real.

"I'll just be in the office while you two catch up," Spence said rather diplomatically. And he looked a little stunned when his cousin spun around and gave him the more enthusiastic hug she'd almost knocked Hetty over with.

"Thank you for taking such good care of her, Spence."

"I'm not—"

"Hush," Hetty said to him, startling him anew. "You are and you have."

And she thought the combination of his embarrassed expression and the heat that flashed in those gorgeous blue eyes of his was the most wonderful thing she'd ever seen.

When they were alone, Lakin ushered her to the seating area in the lobby. Hetty took one of the armchairs across from the sofa, since the seat was higher and it would be easier for her to get up. Lakin sat on the edge of the coffee table, as if she needed to be closer to her. Hetty noticed, and felt a renewed rush of the warmth she always felt toward this friend she so much wanted to be family. Yes, Troy better get his act together.

They talked about that for a bit, but not long since it was old ground they'd been over many times. Then Lakin caught her up on the doings at RTA, including how they'd rented a floatplane temporarily until the one she normally flew was fully repaired, and how her dad was saying after only two weeks of filling in that they needed to give Hetty a raise.

Hetty laughed at that. "They just gave me one six months ago. A healthy one, too."

"They want you happy and staying," Lakin said fervently. "Even more now that we're limping along without you." A grin flashed across her face. "And with you."

"I'll be back soon, I swear." *And that's to myself as much as anyone. No matter how much it hurts, I'll push through.*

Lakin glanced at the closed office door then back to Hetty. "Maybe, in the end, this will have been a good thing." Hetty blinked and Lakin went on hastily. "I mean you and Spence... I'm not imagining things have changed between you, am I?"

"I...no. Not, you're not." Somehow admitting it out loud to Lakin made it even more real to her.

Her friend hesitated, but Hetty could tell by her wrinkled brow she was on the verge of saying more.

"Out with it, girlfriend," she said.

"I just… I know it's none of my business, but you've always been there for me about Troy and…" Hetty stayed silent, knowing Lakin would get there. And when she did, it came out in a rush. "You're sure it's not just…what happened? I know crazy feelings can happen when you go through something like that together. And my brother Eli has talked about how all that danger, and tension, and the rush of relief when you survive can skew your thinking and your emotions."

Hetty stared at her friend. "You think…it's not real?"

"Oh, no, and I hope it is!" Lakin took a deep breath. "I've always thought there was something else behind all the annoyance and the little jabs you fired at him. I just don't want either you or my cousin hurt."

Hetty leaned forward, ignoring the tug from her leg, until she could take Lakin's hand in hers. "My brother is a very lucky man. And he'd better wake up darn soon or my next therapy exercise is going to be to kick his butt."

Lakin laughed and could barely stop to say, "I want to watch that."

"I'll be selling tickets," Hetty promised.

Yes, she was going to be having a long talk with Troy when he finally got that butt she was going to kick off that oil rig.

Chapter 31

It had been a bit of a rough ride on the ATV, but Hetty gauged the slightly increased ache in her leg and labeled it worth it.

But then, this spot would be worth almost anything. And Spence had said it wasn't even in the top three on his list, so she couldn't even imagine what incredible place held that number-one spot.

He'd arranged his work schedule so that he had time to make this trek. Changed everything for her, as he had for days on end now. She knew he had made a run to take some regulars up to one of the family-style camps they had set up this Friday morning, but didn't have to go back for them until Sunday afternoon. And so here they were, in this place she'd never been and that he apparently never shared.

Until now.

It was strange, she'd always thought she had the best views possible of this beautiful land she lived in. Because what could be better than flying high above it, able to see for miles and miles in all directions? What could be better than truly realizing the size and scope of this state she loved, which was bigger than the next three largest states combined?

But she had overlooked the things she didn't get from altitude, from her plane. The caress of a summer breeze, the scent of things growing so madly fast since they had so little time, the vibrant life of the birds and animals making the most of this short season.

The distinctive calls of a pair of bald eagles, talking to each other, cut through the silence that she'd realized wasn't really silent at all. It had been Spence who had told her to just sit there, quietly.

"Wait and listen," he'd said when they'd reached the top of the rise that overlooked their hometown in one direction and a small verdant hillside in the other. She had, and soon had realized she could hear the rustle of leaves and branches where there was no wind, the differing calls of so many birds and, as they'd waited, eventually the chatter of other, grounded creatures also making the most of the sunshine and warmth.

Things she was never aware of from the cockpit of an airplane. She'd been so busy flying over this land, she'd forgotten the wonder of walking it. She wouldn't let that happen again.

Hetty smiled inwardly as she thought that Spence would see to that.

"Thank you," she said softly, not wanting to disturb their temporary neighbors. "I'd forgotten how different it is...down here."

"If you only see the big picture all the time, you can miss the little details that make it worth it." Spence spoke as quietly as she had, barely above a whisper, but with the rough edge that made her skin tingle.

"I'm realizing that," she answered. Then, with a smile,

she added, "They must be used to you, the locals up here. They barely turned a hair—or a feather—when we motored up to this spot."

He gave her a smile. That slightly crooked one she treasured. "They are, I think. This is my closest secret spot, so it's the one I come to when I need the break but don't have time for one of the others."

"Will you show me those, too? When I can make it that far?"

"Everything," he said in the tone of a vow. "No secrets, not from you."

Her throat tightened. When Spence Colton made up his mind, he obviously didn't do it halfway.

"Well," she said, turning in the ATV's surprisingly comfortable seat to look straight at him, "in that same vein of no secrets, I had a little chat with my doctor this morning."

Spence went very still. He of course knew she'd been for a follow-up, since he'd been the one to take her there.

"Not bad news?" he asked, sounding rather endearingly anxious.

"The opposite. She said I'm healing well, and that if I'm careful, I can do anything I feel up to, short of climbing Denali."

"Well, darn," Spence said, grinning with obvious relief now, "there go my plans for us for the weekend."

She took a deep breath. She wasn't sure why this was so difficult. The man had been taking care of her for three weeks straight, and once how he felt about her was out in the open, he'd apparently had no qualms about admitting it. And she'd confronted her feelings for him while she was still lying in that hospital, watching him sleep restlessly in the chair beside her bed.

"I was hoping we could make other plans for the weekend," she managed to get out, feeling heat rising up to her cheeks.

"Sure," he said cheerfully. "Where do you want to go?"

She needed another deep breath. Wondered if she was jumping the gun, if it was too soon, if she had misinterpreted—

"Hetty?"

She met his gaze, stared into those eyes she knew so well. "I've never been to your place."

"I know, you never wanted to—" He broke off and she saw his eyes widen. He swallowed visibly. "Hetty?"

"You've been in and out of my place picking things up for me for three weeks now. Don't you think it's time I saw yours?"

"I...sure."

He looked a little nervous and she wondered if it was because he was a guy nervous about what mess he might have left behind, or if he'd read her intent. Her intent that the tour would end in his bedroom. She'd waited long enough, and the doctor had indeed said, if she was careful, it would be all right.

"Just let him do all the work," she'd said in a teasing tone that made Hetty like her even more. She'd even dug into a supply drawer and come up with a box of condoms, which she'd tossed to Hetty with a grin. That box was now tucked away in her purse, which was locked in his SUV back at RTA where they'd picked up their ride.

* * *

Spence's home was nothing like she'd imagined. The cabin-like two-bedroom place not far from the RTA office had large windows facing downhill toward the sound. To the rear, it was tucked into a stand of trees, and knowing Spence's penchant for being outside whenever possible, she'd bet there was a deck out there.

The inside was…cozy. Warm. Welcoming. She thought she recognized Abby Colton's fine hand in the décor, but the color scheme was pure Spence: evergreen, blue, and the gray of a young Sitka spruce. Like the one masking the cave.

And it was tidy. Tidier than her own place sometimes got. Sure, there were some boots by the door, but that was typical of just about anyone up here. There was a jacket tossed over the back of a chair, and an empty coffee mug on the counter between the kitchen and the living room, but other than that, if there was a mess, it was hidden.

In the bedroom?

She wondered when Spence Colton's bedroom had become the focus of her existence. That night in the cave? Or when he'd kissed her in his parents' house? Or when Dr. Masters had given her the okay to…what? Jump him? No, she was supposed to let him do all the work.

Her pulse kicked up at the images that brought to mind. Trying to slow herself down, she looked around the living room. Her gaze stopped dead at the unexpected item on the wall above the couch. A large, framed photograph of, of all things, a big city. She scanned for any landmarks she'd recognize that would tell her what megametropolis it was, but found nothing.

Finally, she looked at Spence. "Well, that was the last thing I would have expected to see on your wall."

He started to respond but stopped. Then the words finally came. "You want to know why?"

She went very still inside, sensing there was much more to this than the surface question. "I want to know everything," she said quietly.

She saw him swallow, as if her words had reached him beyond their mere definition. It was a moment before he said, "It's all about the sequence."

She blinked, not understanding. Instead of explaining in more words, he walked toward the couch. She made herself look at more than just the way he moved, and saw he was looking at the picture. When he reached the couch, he turned around and sat down. And was, she realized, facing the large windows with the spectacular view down to the sound, with the mountains on the other side sharp and clear on this cloudless day. If anything, an image of that panorama was what she would have expected to see on his wall.

It's all about the sequence.

It hit her then. He'd walked over facing the city and then…turned his back on it. Turned to face the reality outside. His reality, the place and the life he loved.

"It's there to remind you how glad you are to live here," she said.

"And not there," he said. "I knew you'd get it. Because you get me."

"More now," she admitted.

To her surprise, he shook his head. "You got me back when I needed it most."

She knew he meant back in school. "I always knew how

smart you were, you just had this glitch. It took until I realized how brilliant you were at math, unless it was a word problem, to put it together."

"But you did. I thought I was just stupid, like everybody said."

"Surely your parents didn't."

He shrugged and looked a little sheepish. "No, they didn't. They told me just the opposite. But at that age, what do your parents know?"

She laughed. "I was always amazed at how smart Mom got after I turned twenty-five."

"Yes. Mine, too."

"They are very smart," she confirmed.

"But they think…" He shifted his gaze back to the window.

"They think what?"

"That we…belong." He looked back at her, took a deep breath and added, "Together."

And there it was. The opening she'd wanted. And, for the first time, she didn't hesitate. "Told you they were smart."

"Hetty…"

"I'd run to you, like in the movies, if I could."

He was on his feet in an instant. He didn't quite run, but only because the room wasn't that big. Still, he was with her in mere seconds, close, warm, his arms around her as he looked down at her.

"You're sure, Hetty? Because if you change your mind, I'll stop, but it may kill me."

She smiled up at him, letting all the feelings that had been swirling between them show. "When do I get to see the bedroom?"

He swore under his breath, low, harsh, and so hungry, it made her flush with heat.

"By the way," she added, feeling a little giddy, "the doctor says you have to do all the work."

"My pleasure," he said, and he sounded every bit as hot and eager as she felt.

The promise of that night in the cave was about to be kept.

Chapter 32

Spence wasn't a slob, something he was thankful for at the moment. He might have tossed a shirt over the back of that chair by the window and hung the towel to dry from the bathroom doorknob this morning, but other than that, the bedroom was tidy enough. Besides, to him, the big window that looked down at the sound, and the fact that he could see just the edge of the RTA building in the distance, made him not care so much what the inside looked like. Of course, it made life a little interesting this time of year when the sun never really set, but a good pair of blackout curtains helped.

But right now, absolutely nothing mattered other than the woman he held in his arms. He'd never dreamed, never dared even hoped, that they might end up here like this someday. He'd always thought she'd disliked him so much it could never, ever, happen. He'd always thought she still remembered him as that kid everyone wrote off as stupid, or whose brain was weird.

And then he couldn't think at all because Hetty, his Hetty, the woman he'd always assumed was far beyond his reach, was kissing him. Hotly, fiercely, until he was breathless. He had the crazy thought his muscles had melted from it, because he felt as if they couldn't hold him up any longer.

It was all he could do to control how they fell onto his bed, making sure he took the brunt, with Hetty deliciously on top of him. She was so lithe, energetic and strong, he almost forgot about her leg. And the doctor's orders.

He tore his mouth from hers long enough to say, "I'm supposed to be doing all the work, remember?"

"Then stop being so hot," she whispered.

Spence didn't know whether to laugh or yell with joy, and what came out was a tangle of both. Clothes disappeared in a rush and it was all he could do to handle hers gently, although when she was fully healed and well, all bets would be off. He fumbled with the condom. He would have written it off to it having been a while, but he had the feeling it was just Hetty.

His imaginings of how this might be, if it ever came to pass, were nothing compared to the living, breathing reality. Fiery was the only word he could think of. Every time he touched her, heat leapt along his nerves, and when she touched him, it roared to life so fiercely he was surprised he couldn't hear the crackle of the flames.

What he did hear were the small sounds she made. A moan here, a gasp there, to a cry out loud when he found one of those places on her body that did the same thing to her that she was doing to him. He memorized every single one. Because he planned to visit them again and again and again.

But then she slid her hands down his back, cupping his backside and pushing, as if she wanted him even closer.

"Can we hurry this time and go slower next time?" he

asked hoarsely, not sure how he was going to stand it if she said no.

"I think…" she began, stopping for another little gasp as he gave a nipple a gentle squeeze. "We'd better hurry two or three times. Then maybe I can slow down."

With that, she shifted a hand to reach between them, wrapping her fingers around that part of him that had paid attention to her since they were sixteen. He groaned, low and harsh, gritting his teeth to keep from exploding. She guided him and he let her, but when he felt the slick heat of her, he couldn't wait. He slid into her with a muttered oath, and at her cry of pleasure at the invasion, he nearly lost it right then.

On some level, he knew there would never be another time like this first time. And in a way he was glad, because this was going to be embarrassingly quick. But any embarrassment vanished as, on his fifth, long, driving stroke, she cried out his name and bucked beneath him, her body clenching around him until he cried out as it engulfed him and he spiraled upward with her.

In the quiet aftermath, as he shifted so he could hold her gently, even now aware of her injury, he realized none of his teenage imaginings had even come close.

Spence had always liked this little home of his. He was grateful for the amount of space, which was enough but not too much, appreciated the pieces Mom had helped him pick out, and the colors that, for him anyway, brought the outside in. Because the outside was what he loved the most. Half hidden in the trees, with the secluded feel, while keeping that glorious view, yet he was just a short distance from work. For him, the best of both worlds.

At least, he'd thought it the best. He realized it had only been good. Now that Hetty was here, it had moved up to the best.

It had moved up to more than he had ever imagined. He supposed a week of heaven would do that to you. A week of realizing that his imagination had fallen far short of reality. Because being with Hetty, touching her, making love to her, had made him feel things he'd never realized were possible.

And he had the sneaking suspicion, awkward as it was, that he understood his parents a little better now. The fact that he could think of himself and Hetty together in the same way he thought of that rock-solid couple who had built this life after tragedy only confirmed what he was feeling.

This was it.

This was his forever.

He was smiling as they sat out on his front porch, sipping hot chocolate while watching a pair of eagles atop a tall cedar tree to the west. They'd alternated between sitting out here with the view down to the water and the back deck that looked out to the thick trees. The fact that it had been Hetty's idea only proved his feelings right. She got it; she understood the appeal of both the expansive view and the secluded ambience of the tall trees.

The eagles took off, one after the other, their calls to each other loud and clear and as distinctive as the striking white head and tail against the dark brown body.

"They're unmistakable not just in looks, aren't they?" Hetty said.

He looked at her then, as once more she'd mirrored his

own thoughts. He wondered if it had always been like that, if she'd always been thinking what he was thinking and they'd just never known it because of that wall they'd built between them.

That wall that had been utterly and thoroughly destroyed in the last week. The wall he wanted to make sure was never, ever, rebuilt.

"Yes. And appropriately regal."

She smiled. "That, too."

"And noble. They mate for life, you know."

She gave him a look he couldn't read. But all she said was, "I did know."

For a moment, he was worried, but then she let out a sigh that sounded utterly relaxed. And she wasn't, as she had once been after her therapy sessions, rubbing at her healing leg. She was merely sitting, enjoying.

"So, therapy went well today? You don't seem as sore."

"I'm not. Enough that Liz said I could do whatever I felt up to, as long as I went slow and careful."

He couldn't help the satisfied smile that curved his mouth. "I think we've accomplished that this week."

Hetty laughed, and it was that light, lovely sound he'd rarely heard in his presence before. "I'd tell you to quit grinning like a Cheshire cat if I wasn't pretty sure I'm wearing the same expression."

"You are," he said, not even trying to hide his delight.

He reached out and grabbed her hand, held it, suddenly needing the contact. Visions of this last week rolled through his mind until he had to consciously divert his thoughts, because he was about ready to cart her back to the bedroom to start all over again, even though after that early morning wake-up call she'd given him, he'd felt so sated he could barely move.

"It's so peaceful here," she murmured. Then, with a look at him and a squeeze of her fingers around his, she quickly added, "Not that I mind your folks. They've been wonderful, taking such good care of me, but…"

"They hover. And fuss," he said, his mouth quirking upward at one corner.

She gave him a relieved smile. "Yes. It's a bit overwhelming sometimes."

"You need this kind of peace."

"I never realized how good it could feel to just…be. To just sit like this and soak it all in."

He had to steady himself before he took the plunge. "So…why don't you stay?"

That stopped her. She'd stared at him a long, silent moment, during which he held his breath, waiting.

"Stay?"

"Here. Where you can have this all the time." When she just kept staring at him, he felt a burst of panic. And turned to the cover he'd used for a lifetime: joking. "I promise not to fuss."

She finally spoke. "Careful, boyo, or you'll wind up with a permanent roommate."

There was no denying the emotion in her voice, even for him, who had a bit left to learn about female emotions. But he risked giving his gut-level response to those glorious words anyway, because, in this moment, the rest of his life seemed to depend on it.

"Exactly," he said.

Chapter 33

Spence handed Hetty the glass he'd poured for her before he sat down beside her on the back deck. Then he held up his own glass full of the sparkling champagne for a toast.

"Here's to progress," he said.

She grinned at him as she clinked her glass against his, and he had the thought that he'd never seen so many smiles from Hetty Amos as he had since she'd essentially moved in here. He took a certain pride in that, even as he was aware that sometimes his face ached from all the unaccustomed smiling he himself was doing all the time.

But her glee today was because she was off not only the loathed crutches, but all pain medications, which would allow her to fly again. Hence the champagne celebration.

The sun was dropping, setting as much as it ever did here this time of year. But soon it would be below the tops of the old, tall trees and they would have at least the appearance of deep twilight, especially with no moon present. He liked the look of it, from this spot.

They sat in silence for a while, soaking up the quiet as they sipped at the bubbly he'd picked up while she'd been in her rehab session. It had been a little embarrassing when the clerk, the rather nosy wife of one of the local town council members, had teased him about having something romantic to celebrate, but he'd just smiled and let her think whatever she'd wanted.

Because it's true.

And the fact that he was drinking this with Hetty still made his pulse rate kick up a notch. He'd been so convinced it would never happen, and if it had taken a near tragedy to do it, then so be it. She'd survived, there'd been no further attacks, and the circumstances had forced them to face what they'd hidden all these years. What was now a living, growing thing between them.

Spence could practically feel the energy radiating from her as she sipped her champagne. She was recovering rapidly now, and he knew she was chomping at the bit to get back in the air. So he made sure he was watching her face when he gave her the last bit of news.

"The replacement glass came in."

She lit up, just as he'd expected. "Finally!"

He shrugged. "Alaska. Nothing gets here fast." Especially not commonly needed airplane parts.

"How long will it take Chuck to—"

"He promised he'd have it installed by this afternoon," he interrupted with a grin.

Hetty let out a whoop. "Then all I need is the doctor's okay."

He clinked his glass against hers again. "Then we'll take it for a ride, just to do it."

"*Yes*," she said, lingering on the word in a way that warmed him. And he liked even more that she didn't question the "we" part of his statement. Like she assumed, of course they would do it together.

"I'll check with Lakin to get a time that won't interfere with anything."

Her joy seemed to ebb a little. "I know this must have really messed up the scheduling—"

"Everybody at RTA is so glad you're okay, nobody cares about a little juggling," he said firmly. "Dad and Uncle Will jumped in, and got almost everything covered. Oh, and when we had to change the Freemont trip, the only thing they wanted to know was if you were going to be all right."

She smiled, and blinked a couple of times, as if tearing up a little. "They're sweet." She swallowed visibly. "You're sweet, too."

"Took you long enough," he said with a wide grin.

"Look who's talking," she shot back, and then they were both laughing.

They sat enjoying the quiet. He loved that about her, too, that she had no problem just sitting and soaking it in. The sight of the various creatures, the scents of summer, the lack of human-generated noise, created the essence of this very special place that was in their blood, their bones.

It was a while before she spoke. "Do you have any close neighbors up the hill through the trees?" She was gesturing toward the thick forest just past the small clearing behind the house.

"Nope. Nearest one's nearly a mile away, and he's at about the same level, just further west."

"But you get hikers and climbers going through?"

His brow furrowed. "Not usually. Nothing up here to draw them, not when there are so many other destination-type trails."

She went silent then, and as he looked at her, she bit the

luscious lower lip of hers, making him want to kiss away whatever had her thinking...whatever she was thinking. Then, belatedly, a possible reason for her questions hit him and his mood shifted like an iceberg breaking off a glacier. But he kept his question simple, not wanting to unnecessarily plant an idea that might destroy this mood.

"Why do you ask?"

"I...saw someone up there—" she nodded toward the trees "—when I first came out here. But he—or she, I couldn't tell—vanished behind that big tree the eagles like to use as a lookout."

Spence felt a chill as cold as an Alaska winter sweep through him. It took everything he had in him not to snap at her to get inside, out of sight. Instead, he asked casually, "So you didn't get a look at whoever it was? Maybe it was the guy from what passes for 'next door' up here."

"No," she said. "It was just a flicker of movement. I could only tell that it was a person, not an animal."

He tried to rein in his gut reaction. "So it wasn't Sasquatch, huh?"

She laughed and suddenly sounded relaxed. "No. Not nearly tall enough."

He held out a hand to her. "Come on. I need to do something."

She looked puzzled, but took his hand. She didn't really need it anymore, her leg was cooperating, but he wanted to be sure he got her inside. Once they were in, he closed and locked the door to the deck. When he turned around, Hetty was staring at him and he knew what he'd done had registered. And he saw the moment in her alert green eyes when she understood.

"You think it's him," she said.

"I don't know. But I'm not taking the chance it is." He walked over to the rack on the wall and took down his Kimber rifle.

"Spence, no!"

He checked the load and grabbed a box of extra rounds from the lower cabinet—for the first time really wishing he'd gone with the .300 Winchester Magnum instead of the standard .308—before he turned around to face her. This was Hetty. He loved her, and he would not lie to her. She wouldn't tolerate it anyway, and he wasn't about to risk this new precious thing in his life.

"I need you to stay inside, Hetty. I'm just going to go look around."

"You can't go out there alone, what if it is him?" She nearly yelped it.

"I'll be fine."

"Like I was?" The difference was that he was on guard now, and armed, but before he could say anything, she was reaching for her jacket. "I'm not some helpless female who can't—"

"I know you're not," he said. "And you're doing great, better every day, but you're not to the point where you can deal with creeping around out there without giving yourself away."

She opened her mouth as if to argue with him. But then she stopped, and he saw the reality, the truth, of what he'd said register. She let out a disgusted sigh. And Spence had the feeling this would not be the last time he'd be glad that reality beat out emotion in her mind. She was special, his Hetty was.

"I hate it that you're right," she muttered. "But I'd only be a hindrance out there."

"Call my folks," he said, more to give her something to do than because he thought this might really be something. "Just tell them you saw something and I'm checking on it, so Dad will be on standby."

She rolled her eyes at him. "If I know your father, he'll be on his way here by the time I get the second sentence out."

In an instant, the atmosphere shifted as he laughed at the pure truth in her words. "You obviously do know him." He leaned in and kissed her cheek before saying, "Which is a good thing. It'll make our life easier."

He saw in her eyes that she'd registered what he'd meant. Definitely *our* life, together.

She walked, still noticeably favoring her left leg, which reinforced his certainty that he was right to make her stay here, over to the counter and grabbed up the two RTA walkie-talkies that sat there.

"Every five minutes," she said in a flat, no-compromising tone.

"Make it ten," he bartered back. "And no voice, if possible. I might need the silence. Two clicks is 'all's okay.' Three is 'tell Dad to hurry.'"

He said the last words jokingly, but Hetty didn't take them that way. He'd never seen a more solemn gaze from her, even when she'd been so hurt. He registered the magnitude of that, wanted to kiss her for it, but there was no time.

"Be careful," she said, and it sounded as if she'd had to force the words out past a lump like the one he felt in his own throat.

"More now than ever," he promised. And meant it. But the bigger promise, made only to himself, but the one he had to keep right now, was that he would do whatever it took to keep her safe.

Still, as he went quietly out the door, he found himself hoping to run into Sasquatch instead of a hitman.

Chapter 34

Spence left out the front door, thinking his quarry might be watching the back of the house, where he must have seen them standing. He walked downhill, quickly, away from where Hetty had seen the man, but only because he knew the edge of the thickest part of the forest curved around the west side of the house and he'd be able to work his way back under cover. He entered the trees there and, once under their cover, started up the hill toward that big tree. Another Sitka spruce, he'd noted when she'd pointed it out. The big evergreen with the very Alaskan name seemed to figure large in their story. Which seemed appropriate, somehow.

It was up to him to see to it their story had a happy ending. Because in all the time he'd lived here, there had never been a trace of another human skulking through those trees. That one would show up now was just too much of a coincidence. Sure, it could be just some lost hiker, but Spence wasn't going to assume that.

He wasn't going to assume anything, not when Hetty's safety could be at stake.

Yet even as he moved through the woods, as quietly as any native to these parts could, he found himself smiling. She was one of a kind, his Hetty. When it came to the crunch, she'd weigh the options and make the right decisions. Just as she had when that engine had quit on them.

For just a few seconds, he let himself think of their life ahead, what it would be like to have her with him all the time. To have her loving him as much as he loved her. To maybe starting a family of their own, with the best examples of their parents to guide them.

He felt a weird sensation he'd never known, because, despite Dad's enthusiasm for grandkids—and the glint in his eye when Spence had told him they were losing their houseguest—he'd never thought about it seriously before. Never imagined what it would be like, to be a father. And now, here he was, heading out to maybe face down a killer, and wondering if their kids would have her green eyes or his blue.

He shook it off and focused on the feeling he'd been lugging around ever since that day she'd been shot. The feeling that it wasn't over yet, that the hired killer wasn't about to leave witnesses behind. He might be a city guy out of his element here, but sooner or later, he could get lucky. And Spence damned well wasn't about to lose what he and Hetty had finally found together. Neither was he willing to spend time that should be spent building the new life he wanted with her in constantly watching their backs.

This needed to end, and now.

He put himself in stealth mode; that way of thinking and moving that he used when he wanted to get closer to some wild, wary creature he wanted to watch. He played it like the very first time he'd come across the lynx family, among the wariest of animals, especially when there were kits to be protected.

I know the feeling now. That need to protect above all else.

And he knew it would apply tenfold to those kids he'd never thought about until now.

He knelt behind a thick cluster of prickly wild rose. He stayed there for several minutes, rifle at the ready but motionless, listening. He closed his eyes for a moment, concentrating on his other senses, a lesson he'd learned early when his father had taught him that even a human's pitifully weak sense of smell could be useful, and how to focus on things other than what he could see.

Spence was about to start moving again when he heard it. A slight rustle then a distinctive snap. Something—or someone—had just stepped on a downed branch, up the hillside.

He knew what his vote was.

Everything changed in that moment. His question had been answered and he was no longer just checking, he was sure. Hetty had been right; she had seen someone out here. And as far as Spence was concerned, the way that person was acting put them in the enemy category. And right now he had only one: the man who had nearly killed Hetty.

He moved slowly, silently, careful about where he made every step. This was like stalking an already-spooked wild thing. It was going to take some time, but the ending—peace and safety—would be worth it. And he had one thing going for him the intruder did not…he knew this ground. This was his own backyard, in essence, and he wasn't about to cede it to some city guy who thought he could just come here and start killing people.

Welcome to Alaska, chump.

He skirted the rocky slope that was far too clear of cover for his comfort. He stayed, as Uncle Will put it, a couple of trees back from the open terrain. He wouldn't assume his quarry hadn't at least glimpsed him, but he would make it as difficult as he could for the guy to find him. Enough to get a bead on him, anyway.

He zeroed in on the spot the sound had come from. Caught a glimpse of metal. Rifle. A hand gripping it.

A left hand. Confirmation.

Spence double-checked his own rifle even though he knew it was ready; a round in the chamber and four in the magazine available to take its place. He'd be taking no chances with this guy, even if he wasn't backcountry smart. The guy had gotten lucky once and it had nearly cost Hetty her life, and him the reason his own life had suddenly become so much more worth living.

And that thought reminded him that he now had a much larger vested interest in staying alive, so he reached for the walkie-talkie and clicked it. Three times.

Tell Dad to hurry.

Almost in that same moment, he heard another rustling up ahead. Wondered for a moment if his target had heard the radio. Decided he didn't care. He was determined now; he was going to take this guy down. He wasn't a big hunter, he never liked killing living creatures, but this was different. In so many ways, this creature had it coming, more than any wild animal who acted only on instincts it couldn't ignore.

And maybe knowing he was now the pursued instead of the pursuer might rattle the guy enough that he'd make a wrong move, a misstep. And out here, that could be the end of you, in more ways than one.

Spence, knowing where the sound had come from, decided to shift his course slightly westward. If he came at him from that direction, the natural instinct for the hitman would be to change course to get farther away rather than to continue up and get closer by coming in from the side. If Spence could push the guy just far enough, what he knew and the killer likely did not was where he'd end up.

It took a few long, agonizing minutes to be sure it had worked, but then he heard another rustle. And—maybe, he couldn't be sure, could only hope—a low sound that might have been a smothered curse.

Spence headed for his next goal, the large boulder just inside the tree line, the one he often joked would end up in his bathroom if it ever let go and rolled down the mountain. Because they were pretty much on a mountain now. While the formation was nowhere near the towering peaks that surrounded them, it was definitely bigger—and steeper—than just a foothill.

He crouched in the shelter of the rock, again tuning in to his surroundings with every sense. He saw and heard nothing. Smell wasn't helping, either. He waited. And waited. Funny how he usually had all the patience in the word for this kind of thing, but now he was antsy as hell and wanted it over. Over and done, so he could get back to Hetty and they could start that new life.

Finally, driven by an urge he could no longer deny, he reached down and grabbed a piece of rock that had over time broken off the big boulder. He hefted it. It was only a little bigger than a baseball, but it weighed a lot more. It would have to do.

He straightened enough to be able to put some power behind it, then hurled the rock out toward where he would be if he hadn't changed direction. But his attention never wavered from his best guess as to where his prey was; he had the rifle trained and ready. And the instant that rock landed with a thud even he could hear from here, a flash of movement proved him right.

He fired. With the ease and speed of long practice, he sent three rounds in quick succession. One where the intruder was now, one in the direction he thought the guy would jump, and one a step back toward where he'd been hiding.

Selection B.

He thought it with grim satisfaction as the man screamed and went down. Now, finally, the hitman was vulnerable, hit himself. Spence started forward, staying in a low crouch in case the guy was still functional. All he'd need was a trigger finger, after all.

Spence heard the scrambling as he neared the spot where he'd seen him. Obviously, silence was no longer an issue since they both knew the other was there. But concealment was, so he made his way from big tree to big tree, figuring that even if a bullet got through all that wood, it would be so slowed down it would only make a dent. That was his theory, anyway.

He readied himself to make the next move. But a sharp, different kind of scream froze him in place. When it was followed by a distinctive, tumbling sound, he risked a look toward the clearing he'd been edging the guy toward. Just in time to see him disappear downhill, rolling like Spence had always imagined that boulder would.

Toward his house.

Toward Hetty.

Without hesitation, he darted from his cover and headed down, sticking to the path along the edge of the rocks, the trail he knew so well. If the guy could somehow still manage to get a shot off, so be it, but he wasn't about to let him get near Hetty again.

The moment he heard the metallic clatter of the man's rifle—an old-model ArmaLite, he guessed from his brief glimpse as it skidded across the rocky terrain—he discarded all caution and scrambled as fast as he could. He suspected that wasn't the only weapon a hitman would carry, but guessed whatever else he had would likely require closer range than the rifle. And he wasn't about to let this jackass get close to Hetty again.

At the bottom of the slope there was a steep drop and he took it as he had before, down on one knee to slide while catching the bottom with his other foot and using the momentum to launch himself into a run. But a moment later, he was slowing because he'd seen the unmoving shape at the base of the rocks. And Spence breathed again, looking at the out-of-action shape, because he was within a few yards of his house.

The downed hitman groaned, so Spence knew he was still alive. He wasn't sure if he was glad he hadn't killed him, or sorry he hadn't. Time for that later. He crept closer and smiled with satisfaction when he realized he'd hit the man's left leg very close to the same spot as he had shot Hetty.

The man didn't move, but Spence was still cautious as he stepped toward him, heeding his father's long-ago advice to never assume. And then that same father appeared on his back deck, his own rifle at the ready. Spence waved him down.

"You got him," Dad said when he got close.

"I started it, the mountain finished it for me."

Dad grinned at him. "So you didn't really need my help."

"Yeah, I did," Spence said, glancing toward the house where Hetty had now emerged onto the deck, looking wonderful, as she always did, to him.

His father studied him for a moment before saying quietly, "So, your mother was right. As usual. You two finally got it together."

He let out a short laugh. "Finally."

"Then let's wind this up," Dad said briskly, taking out his phone. "So we can start making some plans."

It took Spence a moment to realize what he meant, and when he did, it was as if his entire future had just unrolled before his eyes.

He never in his life figured he'd be grinning while calling for medical help for a wounded hitman.

Chapter 35

"He screamed louder than you did, hit in the same place."

Hetty laughed, as much at the happy expression on Spence's face as the words themselves. She was still feeling a little weak, only now it was with relief. The nightmare was over.

They were on the front porch today. She wanted some time to put the memories out of her head. Although she thought she just might hang on to the one of the man who had shot her tumbling down that hillside, and the realization that Spence had done exactly that, shot the hired killer in almost exactly the same place that he had shot her.

"Talked to Officer Reynolds this morning," Spence went on. "He says the guy calling himself Strauss—George Merrick is his real name, by the way, if you want to cross him off your Christmas card list—is singing like the proverbial canary. Reynolds has been on the phone to Portland, and they already have a warrant out for his employer. And our clients are so grateful about how it worked out, they've already rebooked."

"You mean now that you captured the guy who would have killed them?"

Spence didn't speak for a moment. When he did, his voice was very quiet. "I never thought of him like that.

To me, he was always the guy who hurt you. That's all I needed to know."

Hetty couldn't even describe the feelings that welled up inside her when he said things like that. It was as if he'd had all this bottled up inside him all these years, and now that they'd popped the cork, as one of her brothers jokingly said, it just all came bubbling out.

She thought something of those feelings must have showed in her face—in fact, she figured she was probably glowing with them—because he suddenly took on what she'd taken to calling his Serious Spence Look.

"You're walking a lot better..." he began.

"Yes. I still need the cane now and then, but Liz says I'm good to go. Keeping up the exercises and stretching, of course."

"Which you do anyway," Spence pointed out.

"Yes, but I need to focus on it a bit more then I was."

"But...you could do the stairs at the apartment now."

She noticed he'd said "the" and not "your." She thought about all the times when he'd gone there to get something for her, back when the stairs would have been out of the question. Times that had ended with a large portion of her belongings now being here.

Hetty's brain did some figuring and she hoped she was right about where this was going. "I could, if I had to." She met and held his gaze. "Am I going to have to?"

She saw his jaw tense for just a moment and wondered if she was wrong, if she'd misinterpreted where they were in this strangely born relationship.

Then he said, fervently enough that that glow she'd felt

earlier came rushing back, "I hope not. I hope you'll stay. Here. With me. You like the place, don't you?"

She let out a relieved breath. "I like it a lot. I like the setting—minus hired killers tumbling into the backyard, mind you—the view from all sides. I like the way it's laid out. I like the wood, the line of the roof...all of it." She couldn't help herself, she gave him an impish smile before adding, "And I happen to love the owner."

"So...does that mean yes? You'll stay, permanently?"

She wanted to giggle. She hadn't giggled since she was twelve. To cover the silly urge, she put on her most serious expression.

"Well...there would have to be a big change first."

He blinked and she saw that jaw muscle twitch again. She wasn't normally a tease, but it did her heart good to see how nervous he was about this. Because she knew him well enough to know he only got nervous when genuine emotion was involved. Being angry and determined when hunting a killer was one thing, but laying himself open like this was something new to her. And she had to admit, she liked it. And liked even more that it appeared new to him, too.

"What? Tell me, and I'll get it done." His mouth twisted. "Unless the change you want is me moving out."

"Well, that would defeat the purpose, wouldn't it?" she said with a laugh. And decided to quit teasing him. "No, the big change I want is...a bathtub."

He blinked. "A...bathtub?"

"Not that that big shower of yours isn't nice," she said, remembering a certain close encounter that had ended with them both on the tiled floor, wet, slippery and breathless.

"But sometimes I like to have a long soak after a rough day."

He was smiling now. "I think we can arrange that," he said. "Under one condition."

She arched a brow at him. "You're putting conditions on my one request?"

"Yeah. That tub needs to be big enough for two."

Hetty laughed, letting the delight she was feeling spill over. "Oh, yes, it must be."

Luscious images rolled through her mind. What she was thinking must have showed in her face because his expression changed. He wasn't smiling now. He was looking at her as if she were that sunrise over the mountains he loved to watch.

As if he were...awestruck.

She couldn't even find words for how that made her feel. And when he moved toward her, her pulse kicked up, her body went taut, waiting, anticipating, longing for the kiss she knew was coming. She would have thought that by now her physical response might have ebbed a little—they'd certainly been indulging enough—but she was beginning to realize that with Spence it never would.

His lips were just starting to brush hers when a firm knock on the door blew up the mood. She heard Spence swear under his breath, and for some reason—maybe the undercurrent of happiness she was carrying around these days—it made her laugh.

"Could have been worse," she said teasingly. "It could have come ten minutes later and you'd have had to get dressed to go answer."

She'd never heard anyone growl and laugh at the same

time, but Spence managed it. Then, clearly reluctantly, he got up and headed for the door.

"Your timing sucks, cuz," he said.

She couldn't see from where she was on the couch, but there was no mistaking the voice that answered, laughing. "Sorry, but I'm not used to having to think about that yet."

She was on her feet, much more easily now although the cane was still close by, before Eli Colton got in the door. He spotted her and crossed the room quickly. He gave her a quick hug.

"It's good to see you back on your feet again. You look great."

"I'm feeling much better."

"And she'll feel perfect when she gets back in the air," Spence said, coming to stand beside her and slip his arm around her.

"The plane's repaired?" Eli asked.

"Ready to go." Spence tightened his arm around Hetty for a moment. "And a good thing, I think she's ready to take off even without a plane."

She laughed at him, but couldn't deny what he'd said. How could she when she was so wound up it really did feel like she would spin out of control if she didn't get back in the air soon?

"Good job taking out the shooter," Eli said, nodding at Spence.

"It had to be done."

And that, Hetty realized, was the distillation of the man she loved in a simple five words. *It had to be done.* And therefore Spence would do it. She knew deep down that that would apply to anything, that she would always be able to count on him to do what had to be done.

"Would you like some coffee?" she asked, still not quite used to playing hostess here in this house, even though she felt so at home. Because it was home, with Spence here.

"No, thanks," Eli said. "I just stopped by to let you know we got an ID on the woman you found."

Hetty tensed, and Spence immediately held her tighter again.

"Who is she?"

For some reason she liked that he'd used the present tense. It felt like he thought that poor woman was still here, still important. Which was how she'd felt from the moment she'd found her.

"We got a DNA match on an old missing person report. Her name's Phoebe Smith. Her family is over in Cordova, near Orca Inlet. Fishermen, mostly."

"Copper River salmon," Spence said. Hetty knew the species well, and that it was the backbone of the economy over there, the incredible-tasting fish selling in limited batches for very high prices.

"Probably," Eli agreed.

"How did she end up here?" Spence asked. "Cordova is an eighty-mile, twelve-hour ferry ride with that stop in Whittier, even though it's only forty miles away as the eagle—" he glanced at Hetty "—or floatplane flies."

That got him a small smile, despite the subject.

"Came for a job," Eli said. "And rented a room near Roaster's. But when she vanished after a couple of weeks, they assumed she hadn't liked the work there and quit without notice."

"But how did it happen? Who here would do such an awful thing?"

"That's the big question, isn't it?" Eli said. "And, of course, that's assuming it was someone from here and not some sick-headed tourist who happened to be here. And don't even ask me about motive, because right now we don't have a clue."

"Except that she was set up with that ring," Spence said.

She saw his cousin give Spence an appreciative look and a nod. "Yes. Except for that."

Hetty hated to think that there were people like that in the world, let alone here in little Shelby. She loved this town and the idea of some killer roaming around loose made her queasy. She hoped they caught him before her mother came back home; she was already worried enough about her.

Eli promised to keep them updated—he felt they'd earned that, having found the body. But before he left, he gave Hetty a steady, clearly approving look.

"Welcome aboard," he said.

When he'd gone, she looked at Spence. "Welcome aboard?"

"Yeah," Spence said but didn't explain. She was about to push when he derailed her. "Why don't we go take a look at your baby? Maybe a little test run, if it's ready?"

Her heart leapt at the idea of getting airborne again, so she filed Eli's comment away for future questioning. She was so excited at the chance to get back in the sky, she barely noticed the slight ache in her leg.

But that Spence knew and understood was the biggest thrill of all.

Chapter 36

Hetty didn't even need his help climbing aboard. He knew the leg still bothered her by the way she massaged it now and then, but she clearly wasn't going to let it keep her down. In fact, she was just about flying on her own, sans plane, she was so excited. It made him smile. He wanted to see her this way again and again and again. He wanted fifty years of seeing her like this. Hell, sixty or seventy, as long as he was dreaming big.

"Where are we going?" he asked. He had his own goal in mind but didn't want to push her.

"I don't care. Somewhere. Anywhere, as long as I'm flying," she said as she settled into the pilot's seat.

Chuck had done a stellar job; you never would have known the plane had had a couple of bullet holes in it and every wire of the instrument panel hanging loose. Which was why she'd thrown her arms around the startled mechanic when he'd come to see them off.

And not for anything would Spence have missed the look on her face when the entire Colton/RTA crew showed up to see them off.

She didn't say anything about that until they were up. She didn't have to, because what she was feeling was all over her face. For a while, he just watched her, feeling a warmth inside at how happy she was.

You're going to stay that way, he vowed silently.

"I didn't expect everybody to show up like that," she said when they were leveled off at altitude.

"That," he said with no small amount of satisfaction, "is what Eli meant by 'welcome aboard.' You've always been part of the foundation of RTA, Hetty, but you're part of the family, too."

He almost dived right in then, but made himself wait. The time would be right in just a few minutes. So, for those minutes, he just let her fly and soak up the joy of it. She banked here, dropped and climbed there, did all kinds of maneuvers as if she couldn't quite believe her baby was truly fixed. And the smile on her face widened with every perfect response to the controls.

At the same time, she was as alert as ever, watching for other aircraft in the area. And he realized he'd forgotten to tell her something important.

"It's all yours, Hetty," he said.

She gave him a curious look. "What is?"

"Local air space. Dad and Uncle Will put out the word that today would be your first day back in the air and everybody agreed to clear out for you."

She blinked. "What?"

Spence laughed. "You really don't realize how much respect you have around here, do you? But they could only finagle an hour, after that, it's back to watching your back. And sides. Or backside."

That last had just slipped out, teasingly. The kind of smartass remark he once would have made. But he didn't want to change the mood now, so he was relieved when she just gave him a rather arched look and said, "Well, if you want to talk about backsides…"

Spence felt himself flush. Because more than once she'd complimented his, and he'd found there was nothing that made him hotter than her hands on that particular body part as they made love. It took him a few minutes to get his focus back. He tried to ease his tension by jokingly thanking her.

"For what?" she asked with a curious glance.

"For saving me from ever having to fraternize with a customer again. Now I can just tell them to back off because the pilot's my girlfriend."

It got a laugh out of her. "And you can bet I'll be watching," she said, her tone full of teasing warning.

When they reached the point where she'd need to make a direction change, he took the plunge.

"How about we fly back to the lake," he suggested a little cautiously. She gave him a startled glance. "It's always been a favorite place for both of us. I don't want what happened last time to ruin that for us."

The look she gave him then made the caution fade away. Because it was the look that told him he'd said the right thing at the right moment.

"Yes. Oh, yes."

A few minutes later, he caught the reflected shine of the summer sun on the lake, the place where this had begun as a nightmare. He knew they could never erase the memories of what had happened there, but they could make newer, better memories. And he wanted to start that right now.

"Hetty?"

She turned her head to look at him. "I'm glad you wanted

to come here. You're right, we can't let what happened ruin this place for us."

"Then let's make something new happen." He took a deep breath. "I wanted to do this while you're doing what you love, in a place you love, because… I love you, Hetty. And I want us to build a life together, one that is so good that the bad stuff doesn't matter anymore. A forever life."

For a moment, she just stared at him. He was afraid he'd somehow blown it, this most important moment of his life. That he'd said it wrong, or that he'd been wrong all along, that this wasn't for her what it was for him.

But then, sounding almost breathless, Hetty said, "We need to set down."

Fear jabbed at him and he looked at the control panel for any sign of a problem. Had Chuck missed something? Were they going to go through it again, was there—

"Not that, silly," Hetty said, cutting off his careening thoughts. "We need to set down so I can kiss you before I say yes, yes, *yes*!"

Spence breathed again. And didn't even care that he probably had the dopiest expression ever seen on his face.

When they were down safely, she did kiss him, her mouth fierce and possessive. And there, in the precious Alaska summer sun, they put the seal on the deal, hotly, passionately.

Spence knew they were going to build that life. And it wasn't going to be just good.

It was going to be great.

* * * * *